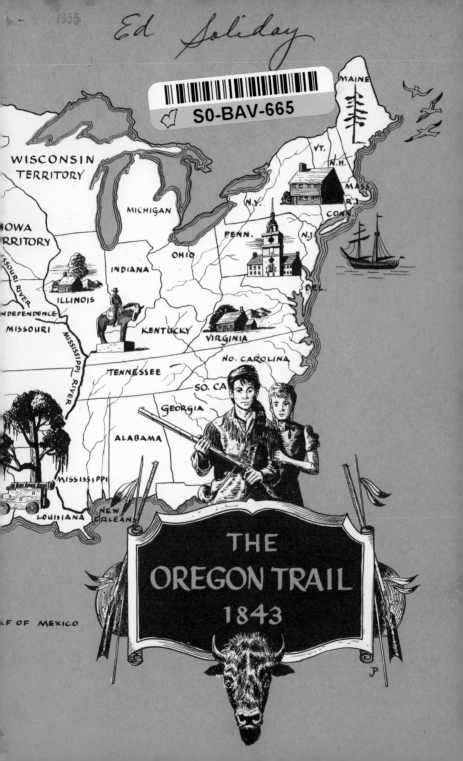

WISCONSIN
TERRITORY

IOWA
TERRITORY

MICHIGAN

MAINE

VT.
N.H.
MASS.
R.I.
CONN.

N.Y.

PENN.

N.J.

DEL.

OHIO

INDIANA

MISSOURI RIVER

INDEPENDENCE

MISSOURI

ILLINOIS

MISSISSIPPI RIVER

KENTUCKY

VIRGINIA

TENNESSEE

NO. CAROLINA

SO. CA.

GEORGIA

ALABAMA

MISSISSIPPI

LOUISIANA

NEW
ORLEANS

GULF OF MEXICO

THE
OREGON TRAIL
1843

We Were There
on the Oregon Trail

We Were There

WITH ILLUSTRATIONS BY JO POLSENO

on the
Oregon Trail

By WILLIAM O. STEELE

Historical Consultant: RAY W. IRWIN

Grosset & Dunlap PUBLISHERS NEW YORK

Printed in the United States of America
Library of Congress Catalog Card No. 56–5042

For

Norman West of the Wild West

Contents

Illustrations

We Were There
on the Oregon Trail

"*I don't believe Pa's dead,*" *Jeff said half aloud*

CHAPTER ONE

Off to Oregon!

JEFFREY HUNT sat in the log barn shelling corn. It was May in Missouri. A warm breeze blew in from the plains, bringing the smell of green buffalo grass and the scent of wild flowers. The boy got up from his seat and moved restlessly toward the door. He stared to the west. Somewhere out there lay Oregon, and somewhere in Oregon his father, too, breathed the warm air of May.

"I don't believe Pa's dead," Jeff said half aloud. "He just can't be."

He went back to shelling corn, finished an ear, and threw the cob into a pile on the dirt floor. Two years ago, in 1841, James Hunt had brought his family to Independence, Missouri, and left them with a farmer named Ebb Matheny. Then he had headed for Oregon to look the country over, to see if it was free of fever, as folks claimed it was, and to find land for a farm. Mrs. Hunt had always been delicate, bothered by chills and fevers, and her husband hoped she would be well and strong in the new country. He hoped for good times for all of them on a new farm in this rich land.

They all had had high hopes when Mr. Hunt left. But two years had gone by and no word had come from him in all that time. No letter, no message, no single thing to tell what had happened to him since he crossed the plains to the West.

"It's this waiting that's so hard," Jeff said to himself. "If Ma would just let me drive the covered wagon to Oregon, I know we could find Pa. But wait awhile, she says. Always wait!"

In anger, he threw a corncob through the doorway.

"Hey," said a voice. "Watch out! You almost hit me." A face showed in the door. It was Corinth, his twelve-year-old sister.

"That's what you get for sneaking up on me," Jeff told her.

"I wasn't sneaking," she said, coming inside the barn. "I came to tell you some news."

Jeff jumped up. "Mr. Matheny brought a letter from Pa when he came back from town!"

Corinth shook her head. "No, but he brought his brother from Connecticut home with him. Now Mr. Matheny says he is ready to leave for Oregon."

"Wow!" yelled Jeff. He grabbed the rifle he had brought with him to shoot at chicken hawks. He raised it to his shoulder, ran out to the yard, and cried, "Bang! Got that Indian. Bang! Killed the biggest buffalo in the land."

"That's fine shooting." Corinth followed, giggling. "Too bad you're not going to get a chance to kill either an Indian or a buffalo."

Jeff looked at her in horror. "You mean Ma has decided not to go to Oregon with Mr. Matheny?"

"Well, Ma didn't do much deciding," Corinth replied solemnly. "Mr. Matheny just about told her to stay here. He's sure Pa's dead. He says Oregon is no place for a sickly woman with two children. He says without a grown man to look after us we'll starve to death or else get killed by Indians."

"A grown man!" Jeff exploded indignantly. "I'm fourteen and I reckon I can handle a wagon, and I can handle this here pretty good, too," he added, patting his rifle.

Corinth laughed. "You're just about the greatest fellow in Missouri," she said sarcastically. "Why, I bet if you saw an Indian out on the plains you'd run just like you ran from that poor reservation Indian last year."

Jeff grinned at his sister. "I had to run that time," he answered. "I pulled off his blanket to see if he had any clothes on underneath it. And he got mad."

Corinth giggled. "Did he have any clothes on?"

"Not a stitch," replied Jeff, grinning. Then he sobered. "But, Corinth, we've got to persuade Ma to go. You want to go to Oregon, don't you?"

"More than anything," she said. "I don't like it here at Matheny's. I want us to have a farm of our own. And we'll have fun on the trip and see a heap of sights. But Jeff, Mr. Matheny thinks Pa is dead, or else we would have heard from him by this time."

"I know he does," Jeff replied. "And I think he's convinced Ma that Pa's dead too. She hasn't said so, but I can tell she thinks he's dead." He turned and looked into Corinth's eyes. "But I don't think so. And you don't either, do you?"

Corinth shook her head. "No, I don't. And I won't think so till somebody proves it to me. I've got to go help Mrs. Matheny pack her dishes now," she said. "I guess the Mathenys will leave day after tomorrow."

She left, and Jeff went back to shelling corn. When he finished, he went out behind the barn to the covered wagon. The canvas top shone white and clean in the sunlight. He ran his hand along the iron rim of the wheels. His father had bought it for them to go to Oregon in. Jeff had kept the wagon in good repair during the two years it had sat unused here behind Mr. Matheny's barn. Now, he stood gazing with pride at it, seeing himself in the driver's seat.

Jeff said aloud, "I believe I'll put some tar on the axles and have the wagon in good running shape, just in case Ma changes her mind about going to Oregon."

That night at the supper table there was little talk. Corinth and Mrs. Matheny passed the big dishes of meat and cooked greens and hot biscuits. There were mugs of hot coffee, and for dessert a pie made from dried apples. Jeff kept watching his mother. He thought her face looked flushed as if she was coming down with a fever. He certainly hoped she wasn't going to have one of her spells.

At last Mr. Matheny pushed back his empty plate and said, "I reckon I won't be getting many more good hot meals like that for a while. Folks are gathering at Elm Grove about fifteen miles from here, getting ready to leave for Oregon. And me and Martha are going with 'em."

Jeff gazed at the big farmer. He liked Mr. Matheny. He was honest and tried to do right, but he always looked on the dark side of things.

"Now that Abner, my brother here, has settled his business in Connecticut and come all the way to Missouri to take over my farm, there ain't a thing to keep me here. I'm heading for Oregon day after tomorrow, come rain or shine."

He looked gravely at the Hunts. "Now, I know your husband planned for me to bring you three with me, Mrs. Hunt. But matters have changed a lot. You might as well admit Jim Hunt is dead. There ain't been a word from him in two years. My advice to you is to stay here with Abner. He's a bachelor and he'll be glad to pay you for help if you'll stay here and work for him. I'll refund the money Jim paid me to see you safely to Oregon, and you'll have a comfortable home here with your children."

Mrs. Hunt hesitated. "Perhaps it is foolish to go—" she began.

But Mr. Matheny interrupted. "It's worse than foolish, it's plumb dangerous. I could look after you on the trail, I reckon. But after we got to Oregon, I wouldn't be able to. And Oregon is a very

dangerous country—no place for a lone woman
with two children.''

"I'm fourteen! I can look after the others!"
cried Jeff hotly.

"You're a good boy, Jeff," said Mr. Matheny
kindly. "Maybe in a few years you'll be able to

come out to Oregon. But not now. Not with your pa dead."

"I don't believe he's dead," Jeff exclaimed, banging the table with his fist. "And I won't believe it!"

"Jeff!" His mother frowned at him.

"I'm sorry, Ma," he said. "But can't both of you see that unless we go to Oregon and find out for sure whether Pa is dead, we'll never know? I believe he's alive and waiting for us. Maybe he just couldn't get a letter to us. More people are headed for Oregon than leaving. Or maybe he was sick and couldn't send a letter. Maybe he needs us. I say we ought to go!" He turned pleading eyes on his mother. "Can't we go, Ma?"

"Jeff, I think we'd better do as Mr. Matheny says," she replied in a low voice. She smiled at her son. "After all, Jeff, you're young and it would be hard on you to drive the wagon and take care of us."

"But I could do it!" Jeff cried out. "And Mr. Matheny will help us if we have trouble. And Ma, I'm old enough to farm. Mr. Matheny knows I am good at plowing and cradling wheat. There's plenty of land in Oregon. Good, rich land, they say. And I know I can take care of you out there."

"Well, if you're going to get land, you'd better get it before the British do," said Abner Matheny. "Back east I heard that if the United States doesn't hurry and send settlers out there, the British will take Oregon."

"Mother, please let's go. We'll be in at the start of a new territory," Jeff said. "The Hunts have always been in the middle of things. Grandpa fought in the Revolution with my rifle. Pa hunted with it in Kentucky. And now I can take it to Oregon with me. Just think, that rifle will have gone from the Atlantic clear across to the Pacific!"

Mrs. Hunt laughed. "Jeff, I declare you ought to be a Senator, the way you talk." She stopped and wrinkled her brow.

"She's thinking about what I said," thought Jeff with beating heart. "She hasn't really made up her mind about Oregon yet. It was Mr. Matheny that did the deciding, like Corinth said." He glanced up to find his sister standing in the kitchen doorway, her eyes on her mother.

"Mr. Matheny," said Mrs. Hunt, "I appreciate your opinion. And I will release you from the bargain my husband made with you. If you don't wish to be responsible for my two children and myself on the Oregon Trail, I understand and will hire somebody else. But I think we'd best go on to Oregon as my husband planned two years ago. What Jeff says is true, Jim may not have been able to get a message to us because of illness or some other reason."

"Hooray!" shouted Jeff, jumping to his feet. "Corinth, did you hear that?"

"Jeff, sit down," commanded Mrs. Hunt.

Jeff sat down quietly, but inside his blood was pounding. He hardly heard Mr. Matheny say, "A bargain is a bargain, Mrs. Hunt, and I'll do the best I can for you on the trail, if that's the way you want it."

CHAPTER TWO

Flash Flood

Two weeks later Jeff was not feeling so proud of driving the four mules which pulled the wagon, as he had been the first few days after joining the Oregon emigrants. Now he'd driven a good hundred miles and he knew it was hard work. Still, he was enjoying himself.

He remembered how wonderful it had been when the two wagons had first reached the meeting place of the Oregon settlers. Jeff had never seen anything like it in his whole life. Children ran screaming between wagons and tents, with dogs barking loudly at their heels. Cows wandered about bellowing. And people were everywhere, in groups, perched on wagons, cooking around campfires.

Mr. Matheny had halted his wagon beside a man

chopping at a tree trunk. The man had looked up and grinned at them. "Welcome to Elm Grove,"

he had said. "I'm cutting up the last elm, so it ain't much of a grove any more."

"We want to go to Oregon with you folks," Mr. Matheny said. "Are we too late?"

"Nope. I guess we got close to a thousand here waiting now," the man said. "Folks are already beginning to call this train the Great Emigration of 1843, but others call us the Oregon Company. I don't reckon it matters either way." He waved his hand toward the camp. "Welcome, the more the merrier. Just pitch your tent anywhere." He went back to chopping.

All had been confusion then, Jeff remembered.

But now they were organized and the wagon train moved west without any trouble. The group the Hunts and Mathenys were with was made up of all those families who owned five cattle or less. This group went first because it moved faster. A short distance behind came the second section. It was made up of those families who had brought more than five cows or oxen with them. But the two groups always stayed near enough to help each other in case of trouble.

Jeff pulled on the lines. "Get up there, Skin-

ner," he called to one of the lead mules. "We got to get to the Big Blue River by tonight."

Corinth sat beside him on the driver's seat. "Do you reckon the water will really be blue and pretty?" she asked. "Blue as indigo dye?"

"What difference does it make?" Jeff asked. "You wouldn't bathe in it anyway. Look at the dirt on your face. And your hair's full of dust."

"Humph," answered Corinth with a toss of her head. "You're so dirty I can see through you."

"That doesn't make sense, stupid," Jeff retorted. "Here, take the lines awhile. Speaking of dust and dirt makes me remember I meant to clean my rifle. It's my turn for guard duty tonight."

"Might as well not carry a rifle with you," Corinth said. "Nothing ever happens. No Indians attack or nothing. Get up there, Skinner," she cried.

One of the mules hinnied and tried to stop. Corinth popped the leather whip over the animal's head and he kept on going into the cloud of dust ahead.

Jeff thought that was the worst part of the trip so far, the dust. Only the wagon at the front of the long train was free of it. The rest breathed it all day. It clogged up the iron thimble where the axle fitted into the wheel. Every night, and sometimes during the noonday stop, Jeff had to lubricate these places with tar.

And the dust was hard on rifles. It got in the working parts and down the barrel and in the powder pan. It took a lot of work just oiling and cleaning his rifle, Jeff reflected. But he didn't mind. He was proud of his rifle and liked to keep it in good condition.

He had met a boy about his own age named Valentine Carter who liked to hunt. The two of them were always on the lookout for something to shoot. So far, they had not seen so much as a prairie chicken among the tall grass alongside the wagon trail.

The wagons reached the Big Blue River late in the afternoon and made camp in an open meadow beside the stream. Mrs. Hunt had slept inside the swaying wagon most of the June day, for she had not felt well since they began the trip. Jeff and Corinth peered through the opening in the canvas that covered the wagon. Mrs. Hunt was already up.

Jeff looked around the wagon proudly. It was smaller than most of the others, but the boxes and barrels were neatly arranged. The things they would need for cooking and sleeping were placed handily on top of the boxes or hung from the ribs that supported the canvas top.

Jeff and Corinth now took these things from the wagon and put them on the grass.

"Ma keeps our wagon as neat as she always kept our house," said Corinth. "But you ought to see poor Mrs. Smith's wagon. She's got seven little children, and boxes and babies and barrels spill out of the wagon every night. It's a mess."

"Well, I'm glad Ma doesn't have a lot of little babies to take care of," said Jeff. "I'm worried that this trip is going to be too hard on her anyway."

He glanced around at his mother, who was now standing by the fire. She looked white and tired. But as she fried the children some bacon she talked cheerfully.

"I told the Mathenys we'd eat by ourselves to-night," she said. "I kind of like to have you two to myself occasionally."

"I reckon Mr. Matheny is just as happy to be shut of us for a bit," commented Corinth.

"He's a good man, Corinth, and don't you fault him," Mrs. Hunt said.

"Oh, I'm not, Ma," Corinth replied. "But he tickles me to death with all his gloomy talk. You know what he told me at noon? That he could tell it was going to blow up a storm tonight, because his leg ached. He said that it probably would be a tornado and kill us all." She giggled.

Jeff scanned the horizon. "Doesn't look like rain to me," he said. "I don't even see a cloud. But if it does rain, I hope it holds off until I get through with the ten-to-twelve guard shift."

"Jeff isn't scared of getting wet," teased Corinth. "It's his precious rifle he's fearing for."

Jeff reached over and pulled his sister's pigtail. She jumped up and pushed him over backwards.

He grabbed her and they began to wrestle on the soft grass.

"Is this a family fight or can an outsider get in it?" asked a voice.

"Children!" exclaimed Mrs. Hunt.

Jeff looked up from the ground to see his friend Valentine Carter. He grinned and got to his feet. "Just teaching my sister a few manners," he said. "Sit down and have some supper with us."

"No, thanks. I just came by to remind you we are on the ten-to-twelve guard tonight," Val said. "My folks are camping by that stand of trees yonder. Come by early for me." He grinned at Corinth. "Good-by, tomboy," he called as he walked away. "You ought to do guard duty too, I think."

After the meal Jeff greased the axles and helped put up the small tent they slept under. Mr. Matheny came over as it was getting dark to see if they were all right. He stayed only a few minutes and then left.

"He still goes to bed with the chickens," laughed Corinth.

"You ought to go to bed now, too," her mother said.

"Ma, you promised me we'd visit some tonight,"

Corinth protested. "Last night, Jeff, we talked with an old woman who was in New Orleans during the battle with the British. She told us about going to the ball given for Andy Jackson, and everything. Oh, it was fun to listen to."

"Female chatter—ugh!" Jeff said contemptuously. "Now men tell some real tales. I heard our guide, John Gantt, tell about hunting with Kit Carson. There was a *real* story to listen to!"

Corinth laughed. "I guess he told of killing a hundred Indians with his left hand and forty-nine buffalo with his right and spitting in the eye of sixty-eleven rattlesnakes and—"

"My goodness, Corinth, you do sound like a tomboy," said Mrs. Hunt with a sigh. "I'm going to bed. Jeff, you ought to get some sleep. You'll be waked before your guard duty. And Corinth, you mend that hole in your dress, then you get to bed, too."

At ten o'clock that night Jeff and Val reported to James W. Nesmith, the orderly sergeant. He kept a list of the guards. "You two young 'uns take the river side of the camp," Mr. Nesmith said. "That's a long strip to patrol, but I have to put the more experienced men to guard the cattle. I don't think you'll have any trouble. Just keep an eye out for thieves. The Kaw Indians ain't mean, but they're apt to steal anything they can. If anybody in the wagons needs help for any reason, one of you come fetch me or John Gantt."

It was dark on the riverbank. Stars were out above them, and shining just as brightly in the water beside them. A fish flopped in the river, and across the stream a frog hollered. Then all was quiet.

The boys walked up and down the riverbank with their rifles on their shoulders. The fires of the travelers went out one by one, until a solitary fire burned among the wagons. It was cool and peaceful after the heat and dust of the day.

The two young guards talked in low tones.

"Do you really think your pa's alive out in Oregon?" asked Val, who had heard about Mr. Hunt from Mr. Matheny.

Jeff nodded. "Yes, and maybe he's found a wonderful place for us to live and farm," he answered. "That's what he went for."

"My pa wants to do that, too," Val answered.

"But Pa says it's also a patriotic duty to go. We mustn't let the British have that fine country. Every American who can ought to journey out there and settle, Pa says."

There was a sudden rumble.

"What's that?" asked Valentine.

"A buffalo herd heading this way, I bet," answered Jeff. To the northwest, the sky lit up faintly. "No, it's thunder and lightning. We're in for a storm."

The thunder grew louder and the lightning brighter. The animals beyond the camp began to stir uneasily. A cow mooed. The boys prowled along the bank restlessly.

"This is awful low ground here," Jeff remarked. "But surely the river won't rise enough to get over its banks. It's probably just a little old thunderstorm. Blow over by the time we go off at twelve."

"Maybe," said the other boy. "Listen, here comes the rain. We'd better get underneath that wagon over there."

The rain hit the camp with fury. The wind screamed and the thunder was deafening. The two boys, wet and cold, stared gloomily from under the wagon. The lightning was as bright as day. What a night for guard duty, Jeff thought. Then he heard a roar. What was it? The next moment, by the glow of a lightning flash, he saw the roiling white waters of the Big Blue. The river had already risen over its low banks and was spreading across the meadow where the Oregon settlers slept!

"It's a flash flood!" Jeff shouted to Val. "Most of the wagons are here on the low ground. The folks have left their possessions scattered around and they'll be washed away. And the people sleeping in tents will be drowned."

"We'll have to warn them!" Val shouted back. The boys crawled out into the driving rain. The river had already reached the wagon that had sheltered them.

"Wake up in there, friend!" cried Jeff above the noise of the storm. "There's a flood. Get your possessions into the wagon."

He and Val began to run toward the next wagon. The water was up to their ankles. The current was cold and strong and swift. It was rising faster and faster. They would have to hurry!

CHAPTER THREE

The Devil's Gullet

THE two boys ran from wagon to wagon, helping the settlers put pots and kettles and blankets and saddles into the covered wagons. Some of the wagon tops had been nearly blown away and men struggled to get the canvas back in place. A dog swam against Jeff and he lifted the wet, shivering animal into the nearest wagon.

The water was waist-deep when Val stopped. He grabbed Jeff by the arm and shouted into his ear. "The water's still rising fast," he said. "I'm worried about my folks. They were near the river. I'm going."

"All right," answered Jeff. "We've helped all we can."

He watched Val wade off in the yellow glow of the lightning. Then he turned toward his own wagon. He was worried about his family, too. The river was rising so fast he wanted to get his mother and sister to higher ground. But where was the Hunts' wagon?

He stopped, bewildered. He didn't know where he was. He'd gotten turned around in the darkness. By the next lightning flash he looked about. There was a wagon just ahead. He'd hold to its wheels till he got his bearings. Out here in the open the strong current was about to wash him away. He fought through the water. Just as he reached the vehicle, the whole sky lit up with great ribbons of lightning. For a moment it was bright as day. And in the sudden light Jeff saw a small figure lean out over the tailgate of the wagon. Then it tumbled into the current.

"Bobby!" shrieked a woman. "Oh, he's fallen into the water!"

In the fading yellow light Jeff saw the woman's horrified face peering out of the wagon. "Bobby! Bobby!" she screamed again.

There was no time to lose. Jeff shoved his rifle into the wagon. "I'll get him," he cried. He turned and dived into the water. He let the current carry him along, feeling all around him as he floated downstream.

Jeff saw a small figure tumble into the current

In the next lightning flash he saw a wagon directly ahead. He tried to stand up so as not to crash into the side of the wagon. But he couldn't get a footing in the current.

The next moment his head hit the wagon wheel with a terrific thump. Jeff thought the blow must have split his skull wide open. He fought to get up out of the water. He could hold his breath no longer. He grabbed a spoke to pull himself up and his hand brushed against something.

It was the little boy. The current had washed him against the wagon wheel as it had Jeff. Quickly Jeff grabbed the child. He scrambled for a foothold. They'd both be drowned if he didn't get above the water soon. With one hand clutching a wheel spoke, he managed to inch his way up. Then he braced his feet against the bottom of the wheel and stood.

He clung there for a few minutes, gulping air into his lungs. "Wow!" he said to himself at last. "I was almost a goner. And I'm afraid this poor little mite is a goner." Quickly he shifted the little boy to his shoulder, letting his head hang down so that the water could run out of his mouth.

Jeff turned around. He was tired. He didn't know how he'd ever make it back to the wagon against such a current. But the boy's mother would be frantic. He had to try. He started off with the child on his shoulder. After what seemed hours to Jeff, he reached the wagon.

"Here's your boy, ma'am," Jeff said as he handed the limp form up to the waiting mother. "He was washed against a wagon wheel downstream. But I don't know whether I got to him soon enough."

He climbed up inside to get his rifle. The mother wrapped the child in blankets and laid him on top of a trunk. She bent over him. Then she turned to Jeff. "He's alive and I thank you," she said. "What's your name? My husband will come and thank you tomorrow."

"That's all right, ma'am," Jeff replied in embarrassment. "I am glad I happened along." He told her his name and left.

With his rifle over his shoulder he splashed through the water once more, searching for his own wagon. Finally he recognized it by the tar streak on the side of the wooden bed. He was glad to see it. What a night this had been—and it was still far from being over! He dropped his rifle over the tailgate and climbed inside.

"Ma! Corinth!" he shouted. "Are you all right?"

"Here we are, Jeff," answered his mother. "We're all right, but cold and wet."

"Who's not?" Jeff replied, wiping his face with an old shirt he found.

"Jeff!" cried Corinth as she climbed over the boxes to him. "I saved the tent. The wind blew it right from over our heads. It was flapping by one tent peg when I grabbed it. I outwrestled it and threw it in the wagon."

"Never mind that," Jeff said impatiently. "We have to get out of here. Right now!"

"Get out!" exclaimed Mrs. Hunt. "But where would we go?"

"Up on the hill near here. The river'll never get that high," Jeff explained.

"Oh, no, Jeff," his mother protested. "We'd be unprotected and the lightning might strike us."

"The river's rising higher," Jeff explained. "It's already over the wheel hubs. It'll soon be seeping through the floor boards."

"But we'll be out of the water on top of the boxes," Corinth said.

"It's not just drowning I'm worried about," Jeff went on. "The current is so strong it might turn our wagon over. It's not as big and heavy as most of the other wagons, you know. And if it were to overturn with you in it, these boxes and barrels would mash you flat."

"I'm ready," said Corinth, picking up a shawl. "I'd rather get wet than mashed any day. Come on, Ma, we'll be all right on the hill."

"I'll come," Mrs. Hunt replied, "but I'd feel much safer right here."

Jeff climbed down and stood waiting in the cold water. "Hurry," he urged. Mrs. Hunt lowered herself over the tailgate. Jeff heard her gasp as she entered the cold stream. Her teeth began to chatter.

Corinth splashed down beside them, saying, "Just the right temperature for bathing. Let's go!"

Jeff took his mother's hand. "Hold on to Corinth," he told her. Then he led the way toward the hill. The current was swift and the ground rough. Corinth and her mother had difficulty with their long skirts which caught the current and threatened to upset them. Once Mrs. Hunt slipped, but Jeff caught her before her head went under the water.

They started off again. "Hurry up, Jeff," Corinth called from the rear.

"If you think you can do any better, you lead," answered Jeff a little snappishly.

"Children, hush! Both of you," Mrs. Hunt said. "I believe the water's getting shallower."

It was. Jeff felt relieved. They were safe. In a moment they were climbing the hillside among the other Oregon settlers. People huddled everywhere under blankets and tents. Some held pieces of canvas or deer hide over their heads.

The Hunts sat down on the wet grass, shivering in the cold rain. Jeff watched the lightning gloomily. It had moved off to the south and the rain was slackening. But he worried that the river might have ruined their wagon and they wouldn't be able to go on to Oregon.

"Oregon had better be a wonderful place," Corinth said in disgust.

"You wanted to do something exciting," Jeff chided. "This is it. Quit complaining."

"This is misery, not excitement," Corinth answered. "I wish morning would come."

"It's never failed to come yet," Jeff retorted.

By the following morning the rain had stopped and the clouds had blown away. The sun came out sparkling on the swollen river. The wagons were all safe. But many possessions had been washed away. And people searched the plains near by for their tents and clothes, blown away when the wind first struck.

The whole day was spent in getting the wagons

ready to travel and in rounding up the scattered animals. But Jeff was so glad the Hunts' wagon was in good shape, and their belongings safe, that he didn't mind the delay.

Then once again the settlers rode west toward Oregon. They had crossed to the west bank of the Big Blue above its junction with the Little Blue River. Now their route lay northwest along the Little Blue River for a week. Then they left this stream and reached the North Platte River. It was easy to drive the mules along the wide, flat valley. Jeff let Corinth handle the reins most of the time. She liked to drive.

The day after they reached the Platte River, it was the Hunts' turn to lead the column of wagons. Each wagon was given a turn to be in front, and so have one day free of dust from the other wagons and teams. But if the lead wagon was not ready at the signal given to leave, that wagon lost its turn. Jeff had risen early so he could have his mules hitched up and ready.

"I'm going to like this," said Corinth as Jeff cracked the whip. The wagon moved off behind the guide, John Gantt, who was on horseback. "A whole day of pure air. Smell that fresh air, Jeff. Isn't it wonderful?" She took a deep breath.

Jeff nodded silently and Corinth went on, "You know, my lungs are just stuffed full of dust. I coughed yesterday and great clouds of dust shot out of my mouth."

Her brother laughed. "What a story!" He turned back to driving.

Corinth looked back as the train followed a slight curve. Behind them stretched the long line of canvas-topped wagons, mostly pulled by oxen. One after another, they rolled across the flat land.

After the wagons came the cattle, which would fall a mile or so behind since they were so slow.

"Whoo—ee, Jeff!" cried Corinth. "Are there really one hundred and fifty wagons in this train? I can see the Applegates' wagon. And yonder's Mr. McClellan's with that rocking chair tied on the side. It looks like the whole of the United States is going to Oregon."

"Here's a fellow who must be coming back," exclaimed Jeff, pointing ahead.

A rider was approaching them. Their guide stopped to talk to the stranger and Jeff stopped the wagon beside them. "Howdy," he called. "Where are you from?"

"From Oregon," the stranger replied, grinning.

"From Oregon!" Corinth exclaimed. "Oh, Jeff, ask him if he knows Pa."

"How's the country out there?" Jeff asked.

"The best," the stranger answered.

"Did you ever hear of a man named Hunt?" Jeff questioned. "He's my pa and we haven't heard from him in some time."

"Hunt," the man on horseback mused. "Why, yes, I know a man named Hunt. He lives at the Devil's Gullet."

"Ma, did you hear that?" called Jeff. "Here's a man who knows Pa."

Mrs. Hunt looked over her children's heads. "Was his name Jim Hunt?" she asked hopefully.

The stranger took off his black hat. "I don't recollect hearing his first name, ma'am," he answered. "But it could well have been. If it's the same one, he was alive and well two months ago. Good day, ma'am," he said as he kicked his horse and rode off.

The Oregon wagons rolled on. At the noon stop

[*41*]

Jeff told Mr. Matheny what the stranger had said.

"Jeff, I don't want to discourage you," the farmer said. "But you tell me this stranger didn't know the first name. Now, Hunt is a pretty com-

mon name. Likely some other Hunt has settled in Oregon."

Jeff nodded and left him. "But all the same," he

told Corinth, "I believe it is Pa, and he's alive."

Corinth nodded. "So do I," she agreed. But looking at Jeff, she wondered. Did Jeff really believe it?

CHAPTER FOUR

Stampede

THE following day the Hunts were the last in line. Jeff and Corinth watched as the guide and three other horsemen rode off. The sun was just rising and the prairie was red as blood. The coolness of the night still lingered, and there was the sweet smell of wet grass in the clean air.

"This is the best part of the whole day," Jeff said.

Corinth nodded. It was nice to sit here and wonder what exciting things would happen today.

The first canvas-topped wagon moved off slowly. The three teams of oxen strained over the rough ground. A man walked beside them. He shouted and whipped the animals and at last got the wagon into the ruts of the trail. The other wagons fell in behind, one by one, until a long line of emigrants stretched westward along the muddy Platte River.

On the side of one wagon a clothesline was stretched with washing hung on it to dry.

"Somebody's clothes are going to get dusty," Jeff remarked, "and they'll have to be washed all over."

"Poor thing!" Corinth exclaimed. "It's so hard to do washing on this journey. Toting water and heating it and scrubbing clothes are mean things to do at the end of a long day's traveling."

A few wagons ahead, one vehicle had a plow tied to the tailgate. The next one had a barrel of water behind. Children looked with sleepy eyes from the wagon in front of the Hunts. Corinth waved to them and they waved back. One of them began to eat a piece of cold johnnycake.

"Who would have thought folks could pick up their possessions and young ones and move like this?" Jeff asked himself. It surprised him every morning as he watched the wagon train move off into the new day. Here was a whole town just rolling across the prairie, here was the beginning of a new state. And he was a part of it. It made him feel good thinking about it.

Dust began to rise from under the oxen's hoofs, dust was thrown into the air by the turning wheels. More and more wagons and animals churned up the dust until finally the leading vehicles could no longer be seen. Jeff turned to his sister and said, "We got to eat more dust than ever today."

"Whoo—ee," Corinth answered, tying her bonnet strings. "I'd love a glass of cold cider right now, instead of dust."

Mrs. Hunt called from inside the wagon, "Corinth, come in here and put this petticoat on." She added in a severe tone, "And I don't want to have to tell you again."

Jeff turned and grinned at his sister. She stuck out her tongue at him and climbed back under the white canvas. "But, Ma, it's too hot to wear two petticoats. I 'most nigh burn up with that other one on," she complained.

"You put it on just the same," Mrs. Hunt replied. She sat down on the seat beside Jeff and said, looking around, "This country seems so empty."

Jeff cracked his whip over the mules' heads. "It sure does," he answered. "And I would hate to live here."

"It's because there aren't any trees," Mrs. Hunt went on. "The land's so flat it just seems to stretch away to the edge of the sky."

"How far have we come from Missouri?" Corinth called from inside the wagon.

"Almost two hundred miles, I reckon," Jeff answered.

"Eighteen hundred miles still to go," said Mrs. Hunt with a sigh. "Five more months of jolting and dust."

"Don't worry, Ma," said Jeff. "When we see our new home and Pa again, you'll forget what a hard journey this was."

Someone's dog ran off to the side of the trail after a badger. Jeff wished he'd had a dog to bring to Oregon to hunt with. Maybe he could get a puppy later. "Get up there, Dodger!" he called.

Corinth had jumped out the rear of the wagon and was now walking along the side. "Don't you want to ride, Corinth?" Jeff asked.

She shook her head. "Riding in that rocking wagon makes me tireder than walking," she replied. She went along barefooted, kicking up the dust. Her long skirt trailed through the patches of stubby buffalo grass.

During the morning Jeff pointed to a group of animals drinking at the river's edge. "Antelopes," he told his mother. "Mr. Gantt calls them goats. They can go like greased lightning. Mr. Gantt says there's nothing can outrun them." As they watched, the animals started up, flicked their tails, and ran off down the riverbank.

They camped for the midday rest near the Platte River. Jeff led his mules down to drink. A tall man was there, watering his oxen. He turned and spoke to the boy.

Jeff didn't know the man's name, but he had seen him around the camp. He liked him because he was quiet and not given to loud talking and bragging. Many of the settlers were big talkers, Jeff noticed.

"How are them mules holding up?" the man asked.

"They're doing all right, so far," Jeff answered.

The man nodded. "Mules are good on short distances," he said. "But oxen are better for a long trip to Oregon. I bet half your wagon is taken up with corn for those critters of yours."

"That's right," Jeff told him. "I noticed not many of the settlers are using mules. But I never thought why."

"That's it," the man went on. "Oxen can live on this hard buffalo grass that grows along here. Mules or horses don't do so good on a diet like that."

"I guess I should have sold the mules and gotten oxen," Jeff said. "But Pa likes to farm with mules. He don't favor oxen for farm work."

The man laughed. "Well, it takes all kinds to make a world, don't it?" He drove his oxen out of the shallow water and off up the bank. Turning back, he said, "If you give out of corn for them mules, let me know. I got some extra I can let you have."

Jeff thanked the man. He sat on the riverbank watching the animals drink and roll in the mud. The Platte wasn't much of a river. It was wide and shallow. No trees grew on the banks, though a few were on small islands.

Jeff was worried about his mules. He was glad the man had told him about their food. He had noticed that mules didn't eat the dried buffalo grass much. He and Corinth would have to cut the best grass at each stopping place to feed the mules. That would make the corn last longer.

That afternoon the settlers sighted their first buffalo. An old bull with six cows galloped up but stopped a short distance away at the sight of the wagon train.

"I wish I had a horse," Jeff told his sister. "I'd ride out there and kill one of those big old buffalo sure."

"Fresh meat would taste good," she replied. "I'm sick of bacon and beans and cornbread."

The next two days they passed more and more small, scattered herds of buffalo. Several of the men rode out toward the animals, but could not get close enough to shoot them.

"Man alive, look at them run!" exclaimed Jeff.

"They're not as fast as those antelopes we've seen," Corinth remarked.

"I never said they were," he pointed out.

"You did," Corinth argued. She argued a lot lately with her brother. There was nothing else to do for entertainment.

Jeff turned toward his sister with his mouth open to say something. Suddenly one of the front wheels dropped into a deep rut and the wagon lurched sidewise, tilting at a sharp angle.

Corinth was thrown against Jeff, knocking him

to the ground. "What's the matter?" called Mrs. Hunt from inside the wagon.

Jeff got to his feet and beat the dust from his clothes. "The front wheel's come off," he answered. "But it's not broken and neither is the axle."

Mrs. Hunt climbed from the wagon. "I declare, Jeff, I thought you could drive better than that," she rebuked him. "Look at the size of that hole. You should have seen it."

Jeff glared at his sister and said, "Yes, ma'am." There were two wagons behind the Hunts'. One belonged to Mr. Matheny. He pulled up alongside Jeff. "Got trouble?" he called out.

"Linchpin broke and the wheel came off," Jeff told him.

Mr. Matheny climbed to the ground. "I'll help you unload so we can get that wheel back on."

The last wagon also pulled to a stop beside the Hunts'. The driver was Sam Roberts, the father of the little boy Jeff had saved in the flash flood.

"I'll give you a hand unloading," he announced.

"That's nice of you, but we don't want to hold you up," Mrs. Hunt said.

Mr. Roberts smiled. "It won't be any trouble to catch up with those slow-moving folks," he told her. "Besides your boy did me a big favor once and I aim to return it."

They all set to work. The wooden chest of clothes was lifted down. Then the barrels of corn and flour, the small cask of black rifle powder, and the many sacks of food were unloaded. The blankets and tools and bars of lead were taken out next, and last, the cooking pots and pans and the box of dishes.

"Now," Mr. Roberts said, "that ought to be light enough for us to lift." He turned to Jeff. "Get that block of wood yonder and let your sister place it under the axle when we lift the front end of the wagon.''

Mr. Matheny and Mr. Roberts took hold of the axle and Jeff stood beside them, ready to lift under the wagon bed. Corinth squatted at the axle end with the piece of log. At a signal they raised the corner of the wagon, and quickly the girl placed the wood under the axle.

Jeff rolled the wheel up and eased it into place. "While you're getting a linchpin, me and Matheny will be loading the wagon," Mr. Roberts said.

"Don't do all the loading," Mrs. Hunt protested. "If you'll just put those heavy barrels back, we can get the lighter things loaded."

A few minutes later, Mr. Roberts rode off to catch the wagon train now far off in the distance. Mr. Matheny asked, "Jeff, can't you find that linchpin?"

Jeff pulled up the top of the box built on the side of the wagon, searching hurriedly through the contents. At that moment there was a low rumble in the distance. Mr. Matheny glanced around. "Look! Is that another storm cloud yonder?" he asked in alarm.

Jeff gazed at the seething mass coming closer. It

looked like black water, but he knew it was a huge herd of buffalo. The ground under his feet began to shake.

"It's buffalo!" he cried. "Corinth, get to loading those things, while I hunt for this linchpin."

"Don't wait here," Mr. Matheny shouted. "You'll be trampled to death."

"Come on," Mrs. Matheny begged from her wagon. "You'll never get loaded and away from here."

"Ma, you and Corinth go with the Mathenys," Jeff commanded as he rummaged through the tools in the box. "I'll make it all right. I'm cer-

tainly not going to leave our wagon and belongings here to be destroyed."

Mrs. Hunt gazed toward the buffalo. She looked
white and strained. "No, Jeff, I'll not go with the
Mathenys," she answered. "I'm sure you'll get the
wagon fixed before the buffalo get here. Corinth
will go with the Mathenys and we'll stay here."

"Ma!" exclaimed Corinth, as she stored a black
cooking pot under the canvas top. "If you make
me go with them, I'll—I'll never wear a petticoat
again!"

"Very well," Mrs. Hunt answered quietly.
"We'll all three stay. Thank you, Mr. Matheny.
You'd better hurry."

Mr. Matheny jumped into the driver's seat. The
cloud of dust and the thunder of hoofs came closer
and closer. "You'll never get away. Please, come
with us," he urged.

Mrs. Hunt and Corinth shook their heads.

Jeff was provoked. He had wanted Corinth and
Mrs. Hunt to go with the Mathenys to be out of
danger. But there was no time to argue now. He
must find the pin.

Mr. Matheny whipped his oxen into a lope and
the wagon pulled away fast.

"Where are those fool pins?" Jeff asked in exasperation, as he hunted frantically through the box.

The noise grew louder. The mules brayed in terror. Jeff glanced fearfully over his shoulder. A great dark, moving mass that stretched unbroken across the horizon was bearing down on them!

CHAPTER FIVE

A Buffalo Hunt

AT LAST Jeff found the short metal pins. "Get the lines and get ready to ride," he yelled to Corinth, who was fastening the tailgate in place.

He knelt beside the wheel and slipped the linchpin into place. Now the wheel would stay on. The mules were snorting with fear and pulling at the traces. He sprang into the driver's seat and took the lines. He hadn't time to go back for the block of wood that had been under the axle.

He cracked the whip and the mules lurched forward eagerly. At once they broke into a gallop. Jeff stood up to watch the trail ahead better. If they hit another rut going this fast, it would be the end of them.

The wagon bumped and swayed from side to side. Once they hit a rock and Jeff felt his throat tighten with fear. The wheels stayed on and the wagon rolled steadily along. But that moving wall of great shaggy buffalo was coming even faster. Jeff looked quickly to the side and was horrified to see how close the beasts were. He shouted at the mules and hit them with the whip. The wagon jolted forward a little faster.

Corinth held on to the seat beside her brother, her eyes wide and her face white, as she watched the buffalo herd coming on. She wished she hadn't teased Jeff. Then he would have kept his eyes on the road and they would now be safe with the other settlers. She peered across the level country and saw in the distance the dust from Mr. Matheny's wagon.

Jeff kept yelling at the mules and they ran as he'd never seen them do before. "I reckon they're as scared as I am," Jeff said to himself. "And I'm scared a-plenty," he admitted.

He kept thinking of stories he'd heard about travelers being trampled to death by herds of buffalo. And he saw himself and his mother and sister falling under the sharp hoofs of the running animals. "Git, Skinner!" he shouted in panic.

Now the noise of the buffalo was so loud that Jeff feared the herd was right on him. Giving a hasty glance over his shoulder, he saw that the black mass was still some way off on the plain.

Could the mules hold out any longer? And would they ever reach the end of that murderous line? It looked as if the buffalo stretched along the whole horizon.

"Can't you go any faster?" asked Corinth. "We'll never get out of the way."

Jeff didn't answer. The wagon swayed so that he had trouble keeping on his feet. He planted his feet wider apart to steady himself and cracked the whip over the mules' heads, again and again. They raced on.

He wondered how his mother was standing the rough ride inside the wagon. It would be much worse in there, but at least you couldn't see how close the buffalo were. That dark approaching line terrified him.

"Yonder's the end of them," shouted Corinth. "Oh, hurry, Jeff!"

He looked around at the charging herd, so close now he could see the leaders' curved horns and the black tongues lolling from their mouths. They were coming toward the wagon like the wind. He whipped the mules, shouting and yelling at each of them.

Then one of the rear mules stumbled. It didn't fall, but the wagon slowed down. Jeff wondered if the mule had injured a leg. He couldn't get the team to speed up again. The rear mule was holding the others back. Corinth picked up the long-handled skillet from the floor board and began to whack the mule with it.

Even through the dust Jeff could see the little brown eyes of the buffalo and the many pounding hard hoofs. But what he saw mostly was that they had nearly passed the herd. A short distance more and the wagon would be out of danger.

Corinth was still beating the rear mule. Suddenly the animal gave a snort and jerked forward. The wagon rolled faster and the team sprinted swiftly ahead to safety.

The buffalo charged past behind the wagon. The noise was terrific. The ground shook. Dust billowed around the wagon so thick, Jeff could not see. He slowed the mules to a walk and slumped exhausted on the seat beside his sister.

"That skillet did the trick," he told Corinth. "But for one awful minute I gave us up for lost."

Corinth giggled. "Ma always says I don't know

how to use a skillet, but she should have seen me then."

Jeff turned and peered back under the canvas. "Are you all right, Ma?" he asked.

Mrs. Hunt, her face stiff and white, came toward Jeff. "I don't really know," she answered. "But I do know I'll never be the same again. What a narrow escape!"

Jeff pulled the wagon to a stop. He and Corinth and Mrs. Hunt had a drink from the water barrel.

The wagon train was just ahead. A man rode toward them on a horse. Jeff recognized the man who had offered him corn for his mules recently. "I take back what I said the other day about your mules," he said. "Those mules can really run. If you'd had oxen, you'd have been trampled to death by that buffalo herd. We all watched you race, and you two showed plenty of spunk. You'll make good neighbors in Oregon." He turned and rode back to his wagon.

Jeff grinned at his sister. "Huh. He doesn't know how scared I was," he said. "I was so scared I forgot we were going to Oregon."

Corinth gave him a haughty look. "Boys scare so easily," she remarked. "I was calm as a May morning." She picked up her bonnet and began to put it on.

Jeff laughed. "If you're so calm, why are your hands shaking? And why are you trying to put your bonnet on backward?" he asked.

Mrs. Hunt laughed, but as Corinth turned away, Jeff whispered, "Anyway, don't start another argument. The last one all but got us killed by buffalo." He waved to Mr. Gantt, who came riding up to see if they were all right. Then the Hunts joined the long line of vehicles.

A week later the wagon train came in sight of Chimney Rock. They had been traveling alongside the Platte River for about three weeks altogether.

Jeff was tired of the wide, muddy river, tired of digging wells along its banks at night to get clean drinking water. It was the poorest excuse for a river he'd ever seen. Because no trees grew along its banks, he and the rest of the travelers had to gather buffalo chips for fuel. He didn't mind collecting the dried animal droppings, they were plentiful. Certainly it was easier than chopping wood. But Jeff thought every riverbank should be lined with trees.

He'd heard that Oregon was full of trees. In his mind he could see his father right this minute chopping down a huge tree in Oregon, lopping off

the branches and splitting the trunks into pun-
cheons for a cabin floor. Jeff wished they'd hurry
up and reach Oregon.

Corinth broke into his thoughts. "Are we ever
going to get to Chimney Rock?" she asked. Ahead
of them a narrow column of rock rose up out of
the flat country. "For two days I've watched that
rock, and still we seem no closer to it."

"Distance is funny in this flat country," Jeff
said. "Things that look close turn out to be far
away. I saw a man shoot at a buffalo the other day.
The animal looked so close, but the bullet kicked
up dust a hundred feet too short of the target."

"Well, I wish we'd reach Chimney Rock," Corinth said. "I'm tired of seeing it. And I'm tired of
the Platte and I'm tired of this flat country."

Jeff nodded. He knew just how his sister felt.
This trip had been hard on all of them and there
were still months of travel ahead.

"You'll feel better when you eat some fresh buffalo meat," Jeff told her. "Val is going to get a
horse for me and we're going hunting when we
stop at Chimney Rock."

"It'll take more than that to perk me up," she
answered wearily. "If Ma should let me pick out a

silk dress with lots of lace trimming and a parasol to match, I wouldn't feel any better."

At last they reached Chimney Rock, a huge mound of reddish stone with a shaft rising from the center. When Val brought Jeff's horse, he said the rock looked more like a haystack with the center pole sticking up than a chimney.

Jeff agreed. "Anyway, it'll keep us from getting lost while we hunt," he added. "You can see it for miles."

Val and Jeff rode away from the rock with a group of six men to hunt buffalo. There were several small herds grazing on the plains. They trotted toward the nearest. The animals continued to graze quietly.

"How come they don't see us and run?" asked Jeff.

"They have weak eyes," answered one of the men. "And they haven't got our scent yet. When they do, we'll have to ride like the devil to catch them."

Jeff kept his eyes on the black figures. There was a huge humped bull off to one side of the others. He would like to shoot that one. He'd never shot a rifle from a galloping horse, but he thought he could do it all right. Loading on the jogging animal's back would be harder, but maybe his first shot would be enough. He'd listened carefully to Mr. Gantt's instructions about hunting.

Suddenly a buffalo raised its head and sniffed the air. "Get after them quick!" shouted one of the men.

They charged the herd at a gallop. One bull raised its tail and with a snort fled before the horsemen. The other buffalo followed at once.

Jeff kicked his horse in the ribs, leaning forward as his mount speeded up. He clutched his rifle tight with one hand and kept his eyes on one of the bulls at the front. It was the biggest one. "That's the buffalo for me," he told himself. "Giddap!" he shouted to his horse.

Faster and faster Jeff went. He'd always liked to hunt. But he had never enjoyed anything like this chase. "This is great," he thought. "Worth all the hard dusty days of traveling."

The man in front of him raised his rifle and fired. A buffalo stumbled and fell to the ground. The man dropped out of the chase to skin his kill. There were other shots now and more men stopping. Jeff kept on. He was going to catch up with that bull and kill it or bust! He urged his horse ahead.

Now he was drawing up on the animal, but he was not close enough to shoot. He whipped his horse with the loose ends of the reins. Slowly he overtook the buffalo. Now he was alongside the beast. He dropped the reins on the horse's neck and raised his rifle. It wasn't going to be easy to aim accurately in the swaying saddle. The guide had told them to aim for a spot just behind the

shoulder, but Jeff couldn't keep the sight on the spot. The gun wobbled and wavered.

But the others had managed. He would, too. He raised himself in the stirrups and took quick aim. He fired and for a moment he thought he'd missed. The buffalo galloped on. Then blood appeared on the dark hide. It wasn't where Jeff had aimed, however, and the wound wasn't going to stop the beast.

The boy clutched his horse with his legs and tried to pour powder from his horn. It spilled all over him, blowing up in his face. The bull was pulling away from him. He had to hurry and get

another shot. He took out a lead ball and a patch and shoved them home with his ramrod. With powder in the pan, the gun was ready to fire again.

He took his time on his second shot. Aiming carefully at a spot just behind the foreleg, he pulled the trigger. The buffalo stumbled, caught itself, and ran on. Then it fell and Jeff rode triumphantly by.

As he turned his horse around, he saw a rider top a rise and speed toward him. It was Val. Jeff waited beside the dead animal.

"Why did you go so far away?" Val asked when he rode up. "Decide to go to Oregon by yourself?"

Jeff smiled and said, "It took me forever to load my rifle for a second shot. I reckon you followed me here by the powder I spilled."

He got down from his horse. "This fool bull wouldn't give up with just one bullet in him. He had to have two."

He walked around the body, gazing in awe at it. "That's a heap of meat," he remarked. "I never realized they grew this big. No wonder they can push over wagons by butting them."

He stood on the animal, rubbed the rough, hairy hump, and felt the curved horns. Once more he walked around the buffalo. "When a fellow's shot one of these, he's really done something. No wonder it took two bullets to kill it. Wait till I tell Corinth how big it was," he bragged.

Val laughed aloud. "You can tell her it was so big it took both of us to see all of it."

"Well, let's get to work and skin it," Jeff said. "I don't know where to begin, do you?"

At that moment there was a whoop. Jeff looked up and felt his stomach knot with terror. A band of Indians on horseback had suddenly appeared, and began to circle the two of them! An arrow smacked into the great beast beside them.

"What'll we do?" Jeff gasped. The boys were out of sight of the rest of the party. Jeff realized he'd been a fool to chase the bull so far away from the others and get them in this tight place.

"Fight for our lives," answered Val.

CHAPTER SIX

Indians!

ANOTHER arrow whizzed by Jeff and plunked into the leather saddle. The horse snorted in fright, turning round and round. Jeff grabbed the dangling reins and tied his mount to the horns of the dead buffalo.

"Get down, Jeff," Val commanded. "Let the horse go. It won't do you any good with arrows sticking through you."

Jeff dropped to the ground and began to load his rifle. Two arrows whistled over their heads. Val raised his rifle. He aimed at one of the riders and fired.

"Missed, by hang!" he muttered. "They're traveling too fast for me to hit 'em. But that fast traveling keeps them from getting good aim at us too—at this distance."

Suddenly, to their right, one of the Indians left the circle and rode toward the boys. Jeff raised his rifle, but as he did so, the savage slipped from his seat and clung to the side of the horse. Only the brave's left foot remained as a target. Jeff was so surprised, he lowered his gun.

Then the horse charged past them, only a few yards away, and arrows began to whip into the ground and the buffalo beside them. "Look out!" screamed Val, throwing himself on the other side of the buffalo.

Jeff took quick aim and fired, hitting the horse. The animal stumbled and fell but rose at once with the Indian still on its back.

As he reloaded, Jeff said, "They shoot from under the horse's neck as they pass. And I don't see how they do it, holding on with just one foot like that." He remembered how hard it had been for him to stay on his horse and load and fire his gun. And he'd had a saddle. The Indians used none.

"Here comes another one," Val said. "Shoot for the horse."

As the horse galloped past, both boys aimed for the animal. The Indian was out of sight, shooting arrows under his steed's neck. One arrow knocked

Val's black hat from his head. Another hit the stock of Jeff's gun as he fired. Val's shot followed quickly.

The horse fell, pitching the rider over its head to the ground. The brave crawled behind the dead horse. Another Indian dashed quickly toward the hidden brave.

Jeff poured in powder hastily and pushed a lead ball down the barrel with his ramrod. He primed the pan. As he raised his rifle, the fallen Indian leaped up behind his rescuer. Jeff shot at them, but they got safely away.

Jeff glanced at the circling redskins as he loaded again. There were about ten of them, he guessed. Most of them had bows and arrows, but two or three clutched rifles. They were naked except for breechclouts and moccasins.

A bullet whined over Jeff's head. That was close, Jeff thought. He was scared. He could feel sweat rolling down his neck and face. An Indian fight wasn't as glorious as the stories he'd heard. Not when the redskins outnumbered you and hid behind their horses so you couldn't shoot them.

He wasn't so frightened that he couldn't keep shooting. But he kept wondering what would happen to Val and him when their powder gave out and they were taken captives. Would they be burned at the stake? Or split open with a tomahawk right here on the plains?

"They're closing in on us," Val said in a tense voice.

Jeff saw that their circle was not as large as it had been at the start of the fight. "Maybe if we keep after their horses, we'll have a chance," he told Val. "I'll get on the opposite side of this buffalo and guard to your rear, and you stay here and watch behind me."

"Good idea," Val nodded.

One of the warriors gave a war whoop. It made Jeff's scalp prickle.

"Look out!" Val called.

Jeff glanced around as a rider whirled past and threw his spear. He rolled to one side. The lance sank into the ground.

"Dang! He nearly got me," Jeff exclaimed, sitting up. He looked at the long shaft, still quivering in the sunlight. A moment ago he'd been sitting right in that very spot.

Suddenly there was a volley of shots from the rise. The boys looked around to find the rest of their party galloping toward the attacking braves. The Indians wheeled their horses about and fled.

The newcomers fired again and one of the Indians fell from his horse.

Jeff stood up, whooping with relief. "Hooray, that's one of the red devils!"

"Hooray for Oregon!" shouted Val.

The men rode up. "Are you all right? We heard the shooting and got here as soon as we could."

"And a good thing you did," Val answered. "They were closing in on us."

Jeff pulled the lance from the ground and looked at it curiously. The steel point was razor sharp. One of the men rode up and said, "Here's a shield to go with your spear. You can show it to your grandchildren some day in Oregon and tell them about your fight."

Jeff grinned at the man. "I almost didn't get to go to Oregon," he said. "Next time I won't ride so far from the others when I'm after buffalo."

The men laughed. "Well, we'd best get our meat and head back to camp."

Jeff didn't try to skin his bull. It was late afternoon now. He cut off some of the hump because the guide had told him it was the best part to eat. He also cut out the tongue and then sliced off strips of the loin. He loaded the meat in the saddlebags, and the larger pieces he tied to the back of the saddle.

Up the rise he rode with the others and into view of Chimney Rock. It looked the same as it had since he'd first seen it on the wagon trail. Rocks didn't change—but folks did. And Jeff knew that he was different.

He'd killed his first buffalo and come through his first Indian battle unharmed. He was half horse and half alligator and maybe just a little bit of snapping turtle! He was a fourteen-year-old boy Oregon would be proud of. He loped toward the wagons, singing a song he'd learned from his father:

" 'Rise you up, my dearest dear, and present to me your
    hand,
    And we'll take a social walk to a far and distant land,
    Where the Hawk shot the Buzzard and the Buzzard shot
    the Crow.
    We'll rally in the canebrake and shoot the Buffalo!

    Shoot the Buffalo! Shoot the Buffalo!
    Rally in the canebrake and shoot the Buffalo!' "

But the leaders of the Oregon emigrants did not feel as happy as Jeff about the skirmish with the Indians. They feared that the Indians might

He was half horse and half alligator

avenge the death of their warrior by attacking the wagon train.

That night the cattle were kept grazing close to the wagon corral, ready to be driven inside the moment an attack started. Mr. Nesmith doubled the guard, and the settlers waited uneasily.

CHAPTER SEVEN

"Prepare to Fight!"

THERE was no attack during the night. When dawn came, the settlers prepared for another day's march as usual. But many were uneasy, and there was none of the loud shouting and joking between families which went on other mornings. Children were kept close to the campfires.

Several blacktail jackrabbits scampered among the grazing horses and frightened them. One of the nervous guards thought the redskins were after the animals. He shouted the alarm, "Indians! Indians!"

The emigrants scattered to their wagons. By the time they had gotten their guns, they found out it was a false alarm. Men picked out their oxen and began to yoke them to the wagons.

After Jeff hitched up the mules, he tied the Indian shield to the side of his wagon. Small, painted figures and strange geometric designs covered the shield.

Corinth was much impressed with her brother's trophies. "What do all those things on the shield mean?" she asked.

Jeff pointed to one of the figures holding a spear. "This means that Jeff Hunt is a great fighter and—" he began.

Corinth turned and climbed to the driver's seat. "I won't listen to you," she retorted. "You get all the fun and tell all the lies. All I do is sit in camp."

Jeff didn't say any more. "Girls don't have much fun," he thought. "But it's not my fault." He felt sorry for Corinth. She liked excitement just as he did himself.

But then he remembered how nearly that spear had put an end to all his fun. "Maybe she's lucky and doesn't know it," he thought.

The wagon train pulled out. Jeff was sore from his long, rough horseback ride. He walked beside the wagon to loosen up his muscles. Corinth drove, and Mrs. Hunt sat beside her.

During the day Jeff picked an armful of purple flowers growing beside the trail. "Here, Ma," he said as he gave them to her, "maybe this will take your mind off your troubles."

"I declare, they're pretty," Mrs. Hunt remarked. "But I'd feel better if these came from my own garden in Oregon."

"Save some seeds, Ma," Corinth suggested. "We'll plant them in Oregon."

Mrs. Hunt smiled at her daughter. "I just might do that."

"Look here, Corinth," Jeff called. "Here's something for you to save for your hope chest." He pointed to several objects and laughed.

Beside the trail lay two discarded featherbeds. Farther on an iron stove sat, looking ridiculous and forlorn. Beside it was a black iron pot with its short feet in the air.

Corinth laughed, too. "I wonder why these things were left here," she said.

"Folks wanted to lighten their wagons," Jeff explained. "That heavy stuff slows down the oxen."

Mrs. Hunt nodded. "I'm glad I learned early to take only what was absolutely needed in a new home. Your father taught me that, always moving from place to place. But I reckon most people find it hard to leave their possessions behind."

The morning was hot and clear. The emigrants pushed on, breathing dust continuously. It ground into their skins, it lay thick on the canvas tops and on the boxes and barrels inside the covered wagons. It was even in their food at noon, gritty and cloying. But in the late afternoon a breeze sprang up, so that the dust blew away and the settlers traveled in more comfort.

Jeff nodded sleepily in the driver's seat. Corinth was inside the wagon, combing her mother's hair. Heat waves shimmered on the wagon tops and on the flat land around them. Heat flashed like molten silver on the Platte River at times.

Jeff woke as a horse galloped along the length of the line of wagons. The rider was Mr. Nesmith. He shouted, as he passed the Hunts' vehicle, "Indians ahead! Form a corral and prepare to fight!"

The guide led the wagons off the trail in a wide arc, so that the first wagon went out and around and back to the trail again. The others followed and a great circle was formed. This was the corral.

"Haw there, Skinner. Haw!" Jeff shouted to the mules. They pulled the wagon to the left, following the others over the bumpy ground.

Corinth stood behind Jeff. "I don't see any Indians," she said.

Jeff beat the mules with the whip. "Giddap, you thick-hided varmints," he shouted.

The wagon ahead stopped and Jeff pulled up close behind. He leaped to the ground and began to unhitch the team. Corinth helped him.

The mules were turned loose inside the circle,

then Jeff connected his wagon to the one in front by the trace chains. The wagon behind was now joined to the Hunts' by chains also. All the animals, both the wagon teams and loose cattle, were in the corral.

Jeff got his rifle from the wagon. "Corinth," he said, handing her a pistol, "take this and shoot the first Indian who tries to come into the wagon."

Corinth took the small weapon determinedly. It was one of a pair Mr. Hunt had owned. He had taken the mate with him to Oregon. "Where are you going?" she asked.

Mrs. Hunt stuck her head from under the canvas top. "Jeff, get in this wagon. I don't want you running off somewhere else," she ordered.

A baby began to cry in a wagon near by. "Hush," soothed its mother. "Your daddy's not going to let the Indians get you."

"You both stay down in the wagon out of the way of stray bullets," Jeff commanded. "I'll be right below you where I can see any Indians sneaking up on our wagon."

He crawled underneath the wagon, banging his head on the tar bucket that hung by its handle from the axletree. Poking his rifle through the wheel spokes, he squinted his eyes and looked toward the west for the Indians. It was hard to see anything with the sun right in your face. Where were the savages?

Then over a rise a figure on horseback appeared in a cloud of dust. Jeff pulled the hammer of his rifle back, sighting carefully along the barrel.

CHAPTER EIGHT

A Sioux Pistol

THE horseman came on. "This will be one Indian I'll hit," Jeff rejoiced to himself.

"Don't shoot, friends!" called out a voice. "These 'coons are mountain men. How about us camping with you for the night?"

"White men!" exclaimed Jeff aloud. He crawled from under the wagon.

"Get back, lad," shouted the man under the next wagon. "It may be a trap."

John Gantt shouted to the stranger, "Come closer to the corral. And remember, there are a hundred guns aimed at you."

The horseman laughed and rode forward. "You folks are awful touchy," he guffawed. He stopped beside John Gantt and stared at him. "Wagh! Lift my scalp if it ain't old John Gantt!" he shouted.

[93]

"Jake Porter!" exclaimed Mr. Gantt. "I haven't seen you since we was on that raid on the Arikara Indian village."

"This 'coon's glad to see you're still alive and kicking," Porter said. He turned and shouted. A moment later, five men rode up.

"Put away your guns," the guide told the settlers. "These are old friends of mine." He led the six men inside the corral.

"Well, I thank the Lord there's to be no fighting," Mrs. Hunt remarked, getting a skillet from the wagon.

"Aw, dang it!" Corinth cried. "I wanted to shoot this pistol at an Indian."

"Corinth! Such language!" Mrs. Hunt scolded her. "And if you're so anxious to do something, take that sack of buffalo chips out of the wagon and start a fire."

Jeff didn't say anything. He knew it was best that they hadn't fought. Some of the settlers might have been killed, maybe Corinth or Ma or himself. And death was a sad thing. He remembered the burial service for a small child a few days ago. It had been terrible to think of that little body alone in the middle of all this prairie, dead and buried and left behind.

"I'll turn the mules out to graze," he told Corinth, "and get some more chips for the fire."

Later, as Mrs. Hunt fried buffalo loin over the fire, she remarked, "Well, I'm glad we're eating and not fighting. I've heard my mother tell of Indian fights in Tennessee. I'm sure I'd die of fright if Indians came after us."

"I reckon old Indian Killer over there is sorry, though," Corinth said. She was making cornbread in a skillet. "I hear that Jeff Hunt is just about the best fighter who ever crossed these plains. Jeff says so himself," she added with a giggle.

Jeff looked up. He was sitting against a wheel, cleaning his rifle. He nodded solemnly at his sister, but there was a twinkle in his eye when he spoke.

"There I was, caught by the redskins on the plains, alone and with only one bullet in my rifle. But did I give up?" he asked, then quickly answered, "No. I made me a round ball of mud and stuck several mirrors in it. Indians like mirrors. And then I rolled it across the plains. The mirrors flashed in the sunlight. All the Indians surrounding me tried to get the mirrors and when they got in a straight line, I shot all of them with my one last bullet."

"What a whopper!" laughed someone behind Jeff.

He gave a start. Then he turned and found Mr. Carter and Mr. Matheny standing there with their rifles. Jeff grinned at them weakly.

"You folks getting along all right?" Mr. Matheny asked. "My oxen have had sore hoofs and I've been doctoring them every night lately. This is the first chance I've had to come over and ask after you."

"We're getting along fine, thank you," Mrs. Hunt replied. "Won't you eat some of the buffalo Jeff killed?"

Mr. Carter shook his head. "We have to report for guard duty." He added with a smile, "Of course, we'd rather hear your son's tall tales. Jeff, I hear these mountain men can tell 'em too. If you can leave off dancing long enough tonight, you might hear some good stories."

"Is there going to be dancing?" asked Corinth with interest.

"Val told me there was," Mr. Carter answered.

walking off. "We have to celebrate winning our big 'fight' today. You two have a good time."

"We will," answered Corinth. She turned to her mother. "Ma, can I wear my cambric dress with the puffed sleeves?" she asked.

Mrs. Hunt nodded. "But don't you stir from here till you've eaten your supper."

Corinth was ready when the fiddle first began to play from across the corral. "Hurry up, Jeff," she called.

"Can't find my peg shoes," her brother answered from within the wagon. "If I'm going to dance with you, I have to protect my toes some way."

At last they left and made their way through the campfires. Away off a coyote howled a lonesome cry. The smell of bacon and coffee rose up from campfires. Overhead the stars shone and sparkled. A greyhound dashed up to Jeff and barked at him.

"Guess the dog smells that lard you slicked your hair down with," Corinth said, giggling.

"I should have put a little on these shoes," Jeff told her. "I never felt such tight, stiff shoes in my life. I may just dance barefooted."

"Not with me, you won't," she said firmly.

The fiddle was playing "Skip to My Lou" as they stepped among the onlookers into the space cleared for dancing. The fiddler was a tall, skinny

man and he sat on a barrel, sawing away for dear life. He held the instrument against his shoulder, glancing around at the girls and winking at them while he played.

When the tune ended, an old man called out, "Get your partners and we'll run a set."

Jeff and Corinth moved into the two lines, opposite each other. The fiddler began playing "Leather Breeches." The caller shouted: "Balance all; bow to your partner, first couple out to the right; do se do and back again—"

Then the tune changed to "The Forked Deer." The fiddler played it faster and faster. Soon the music was so fast that the caller was out of breath.

Still the dancers kept up the jig, Jeff and Corinth among them. One by one the older people dropped out. Then Jeff tripped and fell against his sister, stopping the other young couples.

Several boys rushed up and grabbed Jeff and carried him away from the dance space. "Shoot him," shouted somebody. "He's ruined the dance." Jeff kicked and laughed.

"Feed him to the wolves."

They dropped Jeff in the dust and Val laughed at him. "You'd better stay out of all the dances, you clumsy ox."

Jeff stood, brushing his clothes. "Well, I didn't want to dance anyway. Your pa said these mountain men would tell us stories. Let's find one."

The two boys wandered from fire to fire. Finally they came to a group of men gathered around a man who sat on a saddle, talking. The two boys edged into the circle and dropped to the ground.

Jeff recognized the mountain man's dress of fringed buckskin shirt and pants and Indian moccasins. His face was burned almost black by sun and wind. His hair hung to his shoulders. Jeff had seen men like this in Independence, Missouri.

"I reckon this child has trapped in some far places," the mountaineer told his listeners. "I'll be bound to say I've trapped beaver on the Yellowstone and the Columbia, got many a hundred pack of skins on the Platte and the Arkansas. I've fought Apaches and lifted hair off more'n one Comanche. And I been shot at by a pistol-toting Sioux."

He stopped long enough to light his pipe, then proceeded. "Sioux attacked me and my men before sunrise one morning. A big band of 'em, enough to make me feel mighty queersome. Me and the boys scattered from the firelight. This old horse thought to save his skin by a-crawling down a ravine. I belly-snaked down the gulch, quiet as a mountain lion, and ran smack-dab into a scalping Sioux."

The talker looked around at the group. "I pulled out my knife, quick as a wink, and leaped. But that horse-eating skunk jerked a pistol from somewhere and shot me in the leg."

He pointed to a young boy and said, "Here, young 'un, come feel that there lead ball. I never took the time to dig it out of my leg. Not this old 'coon. He's too tough to bother with a little old pistol ball."

The boy felt the trapper's leg. "Gosh, don't it hurt none?" he asked. The mountain man shook his head.

Another boy spoke up, asking, "But did you kill that Sioux Indian?"

"As sure as my rifle's got hindsights, I killed him," the man went on. "Stuck a knife plumb through his ribs. Took his scalp and his pistol too. Still got the pistol."

He pulled the weapon from his belt. "Here it is, the very same, and don't that shine now?"

Jeff gave a start. It looked like his father's pistol, the mate to the one Corinth had. "I—could I see that pistol, sir?" Jeff asked.

"Sure you can, lad. Here." The man passed the weapon to Jeff.

Jeff looked at the butt and found the initials

Jeff looked at the butt and found the initials J. H.—Jim Hunt! He closed his eyes, feeling the ground sway around him. His father was dead after all. Pa had been killed by an Indian who had taken his pistol!

CHAPTER NINE

Across the North Platte

As he lay in his blanket beside the wagon later that night, Jeff was still dazed by his discovery. His father was dead. It was hard to believe. "I won't believe it," he said to himself determinedly. "I won't."

But the pistol *proved* that Mr. Hunt was dead.

Jeff turned over on his side restlessly. An owl called, "Who cooks for you, who cooks for you-all?" Some of the camp dogs barked. The owl cried again, this time far out over the prairie. Mrs. Hunt stirred in the tent beyond Jeff and moaned softly.

Jeff threw off his blanket. But then he felt chilly and pulled it back over him. He twisted into another position. He couldn't lie still.

If his father was dead, should the Hunts go on to Oregon? Jeff shook his head vigorously. He couldn't think of his father as dead. There must be some other explanation of how the Indian had come by the pistol.

He placed his hands under his head and gazed upward at the sky. The Big Dipper looked bright and close. Out in Oregon, right now, his father might be watching the same constellation.

"Sure he might," Jeff consoled himself. "Sitting there wondering when we're going to arrive."

He rolled over on his left side. He wished he hadn't seen that pistol. He wished he hadn't gone to listen to that mountain man's story. He wished he could go to sleep.

Still the thought went through his head—his father was dead. He groaned to himself and flipped over on his back. At last he slept.

The following morning Mrs. Hunt was not feeling well. Jeff and Corinth made her a pallet in the wagon. She looked pale and there were dark circles under her eyes.

Jeff filled a tin dipper from their cedar water barrel. He handed it to his mother. "You'd better have a drink, Ma, before we start," he said, looking at her anxiously.

Mrs. Hunt drank, then lay back in the wagon with a tired sigh. "I'll be all right," she told them. "Don't worry about me."

The corral broke up and another day of driving began. In a little while Corinth climbed up on the seat beside Jeff. "Ma's asleep," she told her brother. "I hope she's not going to be real sick."

Jeff didn't answer. He couldn't tell his mother

about the pistol now. The shock might make her illness worse.

Corinth babbled all morning about the dance and who was a poor dancer and who wore their best dresses. Jeff answered her absent-mindedly. Finally Corinth turned and nudged her brother. "Wake up!" she cried indignantly. "You haven't listened to a thing I've said all morning."

"Yes, I have," he argued.

"I just that moment asked if frogs grew on trees and you answered, 'Yes,'" Corinth told him. "Are you feeling all right?"

"Yes," he answered. He looked at his sister. Should he tell her about the pistol?

No, he decided, he wouldn't. He wouldn't ask her to share the burden. She was too young. Besides she might let it slip out to her mother.

"I just need some sulfur and molasses," he joked.

Corinth sniffed and Jeff knew she didn't believe him. But he couldn't tell her, much as he wanted to. As soon as Mrs. Hunt was well, he'd tell both of them.

On July fourteenth the emigrants reached Fort Laramie. It was decided that they would stay here a few days to rest their footsore animals as well as themselves.

An army doctor visiting at the fort examined Mrs. Hunt. He bled her, then gave her some pills and prescribed plenty of rest. Corinth and several of the Oregon-bound women took turns nursing her.

Jeff wandered aimlessly about the fort. It was square with a blockhouse at opposite corners. The white adobe walls were fifteen feet high. He stood in the blacksmith's doorway watching the man shape iron shoes for oxen. Several of the Oregon settlers were shoeing their oxen.

On the barren slope behind the fort were lodges of the Sioux Indians. The first night these Indians

danced to drum music for the white settlers. Corinth thought it was wonderful, and any other time Jeff knew he would have enjoyed it also. But he was restless and worried.

He could not make up his mind whether his father was dead or not. The pistol had certainly been in the possession of Indians who could have killed Jim Hunt.

But he might have lost the pistol. Or it might have been stolen. Jeff wanted to keep on hoping. But often at night he felt he was being foolish.

Jeff tried to keep busy. He tightened the bolts on his wagon, greased the wheels, and repacked their possessions. He helped Mr. Matheny wash and cut away the diseased oxen hoofs. Then he

spread tar on the sore places while the farmer singed it with a hot iron.

The settlers pushed off once more along the Platte River. Mrs. Hunt was still sick, but the doctor felt she was well enough to continue the journey.

Jeff was glad to be moving again. Life in the open was more pleasant than life within the confining walls of a fort. As the days went by, Jeff began to feel more and more that the pistol had no significance. His father was surely alive.

By the end of that week Mrs. Hunt had regained her strength. One night Jeff decided the time had come to tell her about the pistol. He picked a night the Mathenys and the Hunts shared supper.

"You two hurry up and finish eating," Mrs. Matheny said to Jeff and her husband. "Mrs. Hunt and I want to do some sewing while there's still light."

She turned to Corinth. "Fetch me that small crock there." She opened the container and said, "Help yourself to these crab-apple pickles. I know you're tired of corned beef, and these pickles make it taste a mite better."

Jeff looked up. "I—er—" he said and then stopped. He didn't know how to begin.

"What is it, Jeff?" Mrs. Hunt asked.

"Ma, a mountain man had Pa's pistol," he blurted out. Then he told the whole story. When he finished, he added, "But it doesn't mean Pa's dead. Pa could have lost the pistol. Or it could have been stolen."

Mr. Matheny picked his teeth thoughtfully. Mrs. Hunt sat very still, her hands tightly clasped in her lap. Corinth glared at her brother and said, "Why didn't you tell me?"

"I didn't want you to be upset," he said. "You were enjoying yourself so much at the dance that night."

"I have never had too much hope that Jim was alive," Mrs. Hunt spoke at last. "To me, this is all the proof I need of his death. He would never have parted with that pistol. It was taken from him by the Indian who killed him."

Mr. Matheny nodded. "That's to my way of thinking," he said.

"Where's the pistol?" asked Corinth.

"That mountain man has it, I guess," Jeff replied miserably. "I never thought to try to get it. I wish I had now. I was so surprised to see Pa's pistol, I couldn't think straight."

"Jeff, you did a foolish thing by waiting so long to tell me," Mrs. Hunt criticized him. "Now we have to keep on until we reach the next fort. Maybe there we can find somebody with whom we can return to Missouri. If you'd spoken out, we could have waited at Fort Laramie and saved time and travel."

"Go back to Missouri!" exclaimed Jeff. "Give up now and go back! That pistol doesn't prove anything." He stopped, swallowing hard.

It was terrible to think of turning back while there was the slightest chance his father was alive. And there *was* a good chance, Jeff felt. His father was capable and courageous. He would know how to take care of himself.

Before Jeff could go on, Mr. Matheny spoke. "There's no need of you returning to Missouri, unless you want to," he told them. "I've been talking with a Mr. Joseph B. Chiles who is taking a group of people to California. He's traveling with our group, but he is turning off the Oregon Trail somewhere ahead. I'm going to California with him. Mr. Chiles says it's easier to get along in California. The climate's better and so is the land. And the Indians are friendly. I believe Jeff could make a go of it there."

Mrs. Hunt put her hands to her head. "I don't know," she said faintly. "I've heard California is fine country. But I don't know."

"Oh, Ma, don't go to California," Jeff begged. "Let's go on to Oregon and find out about Pa once and for all."

Mrs. Hunt took her hands from her head and sat up straight. "We'll argue no more about it," she said firmly. "I won't decide about California until I've talked with Mr. Chiles myself, Mr. Matheny."

When the wagon train reached the fording place of the North Platte, the river was swollen. The train halted while the leaders decided what to do. Jeff went forward along the line of covered wagons to the fording place.

"What's the matter?" he asked a man.

"The river's up, but that's not what's holding us back," the man stated. "John Gantt started across on his horse and almost went under. This place is full of quicksand."

"Quicksand!" Jeff said. "What'll we do?"

At that moment a dignified man rode up and inquired what the trouble was. When he was told, he said, "I'll find a way across."

"Who's that man?" Jeff asked, when the man had gone.

"That's the Oregon missionary, Dr. Marcus Whitman," an onlooker told the boy. "He caught up with our train after we'd crossed the Big Blue River, and he's been traveling with us ever since."

Jeff watched the missionary all day as he rode back and forth across the wide stream, seeking out the best place to cross. He thought he'd never seen a man so calm, so sure of himself, so oblivious to danger.

At last Dr. Whitman ordered the wagons to be chained to each other in one continuous line. "Who will volunteer to be the lead wagon?" Dr. Whitman asked.

Jeff stepped forward. "I will," he answered.

"Drive your wagon up, young man," the missionary told him, "and we'll get started."

"He'll never make it with those mules of his," one man remarked. "It'll take oxen in the lead to get us across safely."

"I noticed most of the oxen balked at crossing the Laramie River a few days ago," Jeff told the man. "Well, I didn't have any trouble with my mules then, and I won't now."

The man grunted but said no more. Jeff drove his wagon to the river's edge. Chains were fastened from its rear to the next wagon.

Mrs. Hunt looked at the wide, muddy river swirling at their feet. "Jeff, I wish you'd let one of the men go first. This is a dangerous business."

Jeff looked at the water as it boiled up and swirled around in whirlpools. Quicksand. He took a firmer grip on the reins and said, "Ma, I believe old Skinner and Dr. Whitman will get us across."

He turned to his sister and remarked with a laugh, "Corinth, get your skillet ready, we may need it again."

Dr. Whitman rode up beside the wagon. "Once you start, keep moving," he told Jeff. "If you slow down at the wrong place, we're all done for. Are you ready, young man?"

Jeff swallowed and replied, "Yes, sir."

"All right, go then!"

Jeff cracked his whip. The wagon slipped down the bank, lurched sidewise, and entered the river. The water came up to the hubs of the wheels. He glanced ahead and couldn't see the other bank. He

The wagon lurched sidewise and entered the river

felt the pull of the river on the wagon. Maybe he had been foolish.

"Jeff, we're sinking in the quicksand!" cried Corinth.

CHAPTER TEN

Rattler at Independence Rock

G ET up, Skinner!" shouted Jeff. The mules floundered around in the water, bumping against each other. Corinth's side of the wagon began to sink. Jeff whipped the mules but still they made no progress. He had to do something quickly.

He dropped the whip on the seat and handed Corinth the lines. He sprang into the water. The mud and sand clutched at his feet. He pulled up one foot and the other sank even farther into the mire.

"Don't stand still, you'll get caught!" screamed Corinth.

Jeff ran then. He was glad he didn't have on any shoes for he would surely have left them behind in the river. As soon as he reached the lead pair of mules, he grabbed Skinner's scanty mane and climbed on the animal's back.

"Come on now, Skinner, get moving." He slapped the mule on the rump. He kicked the mule beside him and the front team quit bumping about and began to strain forward. The other team quieted down. The animals moved ahead slowly, slowly.

Jeff talked to the team, steadying them. Now the mules were moving faster. "We're all right now!" shouted Corinth. Jeff looked back hastily and saw the other wagons entering the river one by one.

The mules were no longer frightened. They pulled strongly. Dr. Whitman splashed up beside

Jeff. "Those are good mules and you handle them well," he praised Jeff. "Keep them coming." He touched his heels to his horse's sides and rode ahead to lead.

Jeff climbed back into the wagon and took the reins from Corinth. "Skinner said to tell you 'hello,' " he grinned.

"That was nice of him," Corinth answered, "but I'd prefer more pulling from Skinner and less talk."

They made it across the river at last and up the bank. Jeff kept going until the last wagon was safely across behind them. Then the wagons were unchained and the caravan pushed on while there was still daylight.

A few days later the wagon train rolled across sage flats to Independence Rock on the Sweetwater River. There they camped.

"Look at the names on the rock," Corinth pointed. "I want to put mine there."

"I can't see why anybody would want to," Mrs. Hunt remarked.

"But Ma, everybody who comes by here does it," Jeff assured her. "Look, there's a large black cross painted on the rock wall over to the right."

"Grown men ought not to do such childish things," Mrs. Hunt said.

"Ma'am, John C. Frémont, a fine man and a great explorer, painted that cross and his name on Independence Rock, just last year," a voice spoke from behind them.

Mrs. Hunt turned and flushed. "Mr. Chiles, how are you? I didn't know anybody was listening to me," she said. She smiled. "Notwithstanding Mr. Frémont's greatness, I hold that names should not be put there in a public place for all to see."

"It's not such a public place," Mr. Chiles answered. "Not a lot of people come by here. And those who do are proud to have served their country by enduring hardships to go into a new territory. They leave their names to show that they are glad to have got this far and to encourage those who come after."

Two men with tar buckets passed, heading for the granite rock. "Mrs. Hunt, those two men are going to inscribe something about your great Oregon Company, with which I've been happy and lucky to travel," Mr. Chiles went on.

"They are?" asked Corinth. "Ma, let us go watch them, if we can't put our names on the rock."

"All right," agreed Mrs. Hunt. "I want to talk to Mr. Chiles about going with him to California." She added with a smile, "And Jeff, put the date beside your name, so folks will know we were among the first to follow this trail."

Jeff grinned at his mother and Mr. Chiles. He turned to his sister and said, "Get the tar bucket, Corinth, while I hunt for the ax."

On the way to the rock, Jeff remarked, "I didn't want to mention it to Ma, but I thought with our names here, Pa might see them sometime and know we had headed west. That is, in case we really do go to California."

Corinth looked at her brother. "Jeff, do you really and truly believe Pa is still alive?"

"I did up to the time I saw his pistol," he told his sister. "Now—well, I'm sort of mixed up."

He turned to Corinth, his face serious. "But I know this. We'll never find out the truth unless we go to Oregon. We can't find out about Pa in California. And that's why we've got to keep Ma from listening to Mr. Chiles and Mr. Matheny."

"I'll help you," Corinth assured her brother. "Oregon sounds better to me than California from the talk I've been hearing." She paused. "But, Jeff, next time you find out something about Pa, don't keep it from me."

"All right, I won't," he told her. She was a good sister, even if she was young and silly. And next time he *would* tell her.

They reached the rock. The two men had already inscribed: "The Oregon Company . . ."

"What else are you going to paint there?" Jeff asked them.

"'The Oregon Company arrived July 26, 1843,'" the man told Jeff. "Does that suit your fancy, young man?"

"It will if you add, 'Jeff Hunt, Indian fighter and president of the Oregon Company,' under it," Corinth remarked, looking slyly at Jeff.

The two men laughed. Jeff took the brush, dripping with tar, and advanced toward his sister. He waved the brush in front of her face. Corinth stepped back. "Don't, Jeff!" she squealed. "You'll get that on me."

Jeff flicked the brush toward her. Tar fell on her dress. "Now see what you've done, Mister Smarty," she cried.

"It's just your old one," Jeff retorted. "Come on. Let's find a place where there are no names."

Corinth scraped the tar from her dress, but two blackish streaks were left. "Boys, boys!" she grumbled. She followed Jeff off to one side. "There's a good place," she pointed. "Climb up on those ledges, if you're not afraid," she added.

"I'm not afraid," Jeff said. "But the ledges aren't very wide." He set the tar bucket on the ground and took the hatchet. "I'll cut our names into the rock and then put tar in it. That way our names will last a long time."

He stuck the ax in his belt and began to make his way up the cliff wall without any difficulty. When he reached a ledge wide enough for him to stand on comfortably, he set to work chopping the letter J in the rock surface. It was harder work than he had expected. Maybe he would just cut their initials.

"Corinth," he called without looking around. "Corinth, I'm just going to put J. and C. Hunt and the date here. Is that all right?"

Silence.

What had happened to Corinth? He looked down quickly. Corinth sat stiffly on a rock in the sunlight, not moving. At her feet coiled a huge rattlesnake. Its mouth was wide open and its tail was a vibrating blur!

CHAPTER ELEVEN

The Big Grizzly

JEFF went cold with fear. The flat, triangular head swayed above its coiled body. The snake was well within striking distance of Corinth's legs. The forked tongue shot in and out between its long, deadly looking fangs.

Shifting his position on the ledge, Jeff raised the hatchet over his head. It was his only weapon— and something must be done quickly!

But what if he missed the snake? If he threw wide of the mark only the slightest bit, the startled snake would strike Corinth at once.

His hand dropped to his side. Maybe he'd better climb down and get closer. The high, whirring sound of the rattlers began again. There wasn't time to get down! He would have to risk missing the snake.

He had to hit that snake!

Jeff wiped the sweat from the palm of his hand. Taking a steady grip on the hatchet, he raised it once again. He drew a deep breath, judging the distance. He would not think of missing. He *had* to hit that snake!

With all his strength he threw. He watched tensely as the blade turned, flashing in the bright sunlight. The snake's head dropped and it began to writhe fiercely. Jeff saw that his hatchet had cut the snake neatly in two.

"Get out of the way, Corinth!" he shouted. "It can still kill you!"

Corinth jumped from the rock and ran toward the cliff.

Jeff climbed down, breathing a sigh of relief. "Wheee, that was mighty close."

Corinth shuddered. "Oh, Jeff, I was so scared!" she cried. "I tried not to move, but I think the rattlesnake wanted the rock I was sitting on to sun itself."

"Do you want to go back to the wagon?" Jeff asked gently. Corinth was trembling, and he felt shaky himself.

"Humph! Do you think I'm silly enough to

faint?" she asked. She drew herself up and retorted, "Well, I'm not. I'm as brave as you any day
of the week. And I'm going up the cliff and help
you finish our names."

Jeff turned away to hide a smile. He knew she
was afraid to stay down on the ground alone. But
he couldn't blame her. Coming that close to cer-
tain death would frighten anybody.

"Come on then," he told her as he began to
climb.

An hour later they had finished. They stood on
the ground, looking up. "J. and C. Hunt, 1843,"
Jeff read and then added, "Looks pretty danged
good, if you ask me."

"It looks like we're somebody important," Corinth said admiringly. "I hope it stays on there forever."

"Well, let's get back to the corral," her brother
said.

"Jeff," Corinth said, grabbing her brother's arm.
"Listen, Jeff. Don't tell Ma about that rattler.
She'd make me stay in the wagon all the rest of the
way to Oregon."

"Aw, Corinth, you know I don't go around telling about everything that happens," he answered.

"I just wanted to make sure," she told him. "And Jeff, thanks for killing that rattler. That was a good throw. And I forgive you now for getting tar on my dress."

"It was nothing a-tall," Jeff grinned. "I would have done the same for Skinner."

"Well!" Corinth exclaimed indignantly. "I might have known you think more of that mule than you do of me!" She flounced off and Jeff followed, grinning.

July faded into August and the train kept moving. Now ahead of them were the ranges of the Rocky Mountains.

"How in creation will we get by those mountains?" Corinth asked, staring at the snowy, cone-shaped peaks to the west.

"We're going to sew wings on our shoulders and fly over," Jeff told her. "But I reckon most of the folks are going through the South Pass. And once through the pass, we'll be drinking water from rivers which flow into the Pacific Ocean. Won't that be something?"

"It sounds like we're almost there," Corinth exclaimed.

"Well, we're not more than halfway, the leaders say," Jeff told her. "And the rest of the way is the hardest part."

Corinth groaned to herself. She was tired of traveling. The newness and the excitement had worn off. When they set out, she had looked forward to seeing strange places, the rivers and the prairies. But the constant jolting of the wagon, the dust and discomfort, had grown very tiresome. She would certainly be glad when it was over.

But Corinth was naturally a cheerful person. Now she found the distant, beautiful mountains interesting. She had never seen such mountains before. She decided to look carefully so that she could tell her grandchildren how she had ridden in a wagon over the Continental Divide.

A few days later Corinth asked, "Well, where is this South Pass you were talking about, Jeff?"

"We've been in it since yesterday," he answered.

Corinth glanced around at the low, flat-topped hills, covered with sagebrush, and at the scattering of trees, and at the mountains on each side in the distance.

"Why this is nothing but a wide valley going through the Rocky Mountains," she remarked. "I'm disappointed. It looks dull as dishwater here."

Jeff pointed ahead of them. A wagon had pulled

to one side. "Mr. Matheny's having trouble. We'd better stop," he said. He drove up behind the Mathenys' wagon.

"Jeff, I've got a locked wheel," Mr. Matheny called to the boy. He watched gloomily as the wagons rolled past. "I guess we'll be left behind. It'll take the rest of the afternoon to unload and grease that wheel and get moving again."

Mr. Carter pulled up behind the Hunts, and Val jumped from the wagon. "Hey, Jeff, what's the matter?" he called.

Jeff told him. Mr. Carter walked up and said, "Mr. Matheny, Val and I will give you a hand."

"That's mighty decent of you, Mr. Carter," the old farmer said. He turned and stared off after the wagons. "We'll never catch up with them," he moaned.

"Why, it won't take long with four of us to work," Mr. Carter said.

"And the cow column hasn't passed us yet," Jeff assured him.

"We'll be left by the cattle section too," Mr. Matheny went on. "I knew something like this would happen when I got up this morning. I just had a feeling this was the day we'd break down. Well, we best get to work. Mrs. Matheny is worried about being left behind."

Jeff looked toward the Carters' wagon. Mrs. Matheny seemed to be having a good time talking with Mrs. Carter and his mother.

He grinned. The old man was worried himself and blaming his wife. Jeff reckoned Mr. Matheny had expected his wagon to break down every day since they had started. He was lucky to have come this far without trouble. And a locked wheel was to be expected once in a while, no matter how careful you were.

They had just finished unloading the Mathenys' possessions when they heard the cattle. "Here come the others," Mr. Matheny said sadly. "I knew they'd get by us before we finished."

The second section of wagons passed by. Then there was a great bawling and bellowing as the cattle walked past. Dust rolled over the three parked wagons. One of the oxen strayed off between the wagons and nibbled at a sagebrush. A horseman rode up and drove the beast back into the great herd. He waved to the emigrants and rode on.

"That's Jesse Applegate," Mr. Carter said. "I

wouldn't be in charge of the cow column for a pile of silver. He and the others have several thousand animals to herd."

After the animals passed and the dust settled, Jeff and Mr. Carter took the wheel off. Jeff lubricated the hub from the tar bucket.

Mr. Matheny walked out to the trail to gaze westward after the departing cattle. He came back to his wagon, shaking his head. "We'll never catch up with them," he groaned. "We'll be caught alone here in the dark, a prey to Indians."

Mr. Matheny picked up the tar bucket and walked away. "Mrs. Matheny will be frightened to death," he went on. "We'll have to reach the corral, even if it means driving half the night."

Mr. Carter winked at the boys and called, "Mr. Matheny, I wasn't through with that tar."

The old farmer came back and set the bucket down apologetically. "I was wondering where the train would camp tonight," he explained.

"I heard a camping place had been picked out at some springs just ahead," Mr. Carter told him. "Can't be far. Why don't you go up on that sand dune over there and see if you can see the camp?"

Mr. Matheny rubbed his hand over his chin. At

last he said, "All right. It would relieve my mind a heap to know if they were camping close." He started through the shoulder-high sagebrush toward the sandy rise a short distance away.

Mr. Carter turned to the boys. "He's too worried to be any help to us," he remarked. "Besides, I noticed the iron rim on his rear wheel is loose. We'll drive some wooden wedges under the rim and that'll fix it for a while. But I don't want him to worry about that too."

The three went back to work. Suddenly they heard a shriek of terror. Jeff looked up, startled. "What's that?"

"It sounded like Matheny," Mr. Carter said with concern.

Then Mr. Matheny dashed through the sage toward the wagons, yelling, "Help! Help!"

Behind him a huge grizzly bear loped, snarling and growling.

CHAPTER TWELVE

California—or Oregon?

VAL sprang for Mr. Matheny's gun lying on top of a chest. He raised it and pulled the trigger. The hammer fell with a metallic click, but there was no report. The gun had not been loaded.

"Where are the bullets?" cried Val, searching among the boxes frantically.

Jeff stood helplessly staring at the bear. His hands were covered with tar, for he had been greasing the wheel. He began automatically to wipe them with a rag.

Mr. Matheny had almost reached the wagons when he fell. "Ohhh, help me!" he screamed pitifully and began to crawl on his hands and knees.

The grizzly reared up on its hind legs, slashing the air with its long, curved claws. It charged the fallen man with an angry roar.

Mr. Carter took a few steps forward. He threw a wooden mallet, which hit the bear in the chest, but the grizzly seemed not to notice the blow.

Corinth was inside the wagon. When Mr. Matheny first yelled for help, she had raised the canvas side and peered out. Seeing the bear, she snatched up her brother's rifle and the pistol.

As she jumped from the vehicle, she saw there was no time to give the rifle to Val or Jeff to shoot. The bear was right on Mr. Matheny, ready to seize the farmer. She would have to shoot the grizzly herself!

She brought the gun up at once. She squinted down the barrel right at the powerful, hairy chest and pulled the trigger.

For a moment the flash in the pan hid the bear. "Oh, I should have let one of the boys shoot!" she thought. "Now I've missed and the bear will kill Mr. Matheny!"

She lowered the rifle. Then she saw the little yellow eyes of the bear as it paused, gazing at her. Had she hit it? The grizzly raked a paw over its chest. When it came away, she saw blood from a wound in the chest.

"Corinth, you fool!" shouted Jeff. "Val, take that rifle!"

The grizzly roared loudly and lumbered forward. It gnashed its teeth and snarled. Corinth dropped the rifle. She cowered back against the wagon. The bear was going to kill her instead of Mr. Matheny.

Her heart beat fearfully as the big beast came nearer. Suddenly she snatched the pistol from the wagon seat where she'd left it when she aimed the rifle. Her hands shook so, she could hardly hold the weapon.

She could hear Jeff shouting. But the bear was so close now, she *couldn't* miss. She steadied her hand and fired!

The bear stopped, staggered, shook its great head. But then it came on!

Corinth screamed then. She tried to climb into the wagon, but she was too weak from fear. Then the bear stumbled and rolled over on its side, dead. Its huge paws with their big yellow claws were almost touching Corinth's feet.

"Corinth, you've killed the grizzly!" shouted Val, slapping her on the shoulder.

The bear was so close now, she couldn't miss

She stared at the large animal, stretched out on the ground. It was a good seven feet in length, she guessed. It was simply enormous and she'd killed it.

She grinned at Val and remarked, "I don't usually take two shots to kill a bear. Guess I'm getting a little old and shaky."

Val whooped with laughter and banged her on the back again. Jeff came up to her. "Are you all right, Corinth?" he asked anxiously.

"Now what did you think would hurt me?" she inquired. "Firing your silly old rifle?" But her voice still shook.

Mr. Matheny rushed up, his face white, his hands trembling. "Corinth, I want to thank you. I would have been killed if it hadn't been for you."

"What's the matter?" cried Mrs. Matheny. She came running around the end of the wagon, followed by Mrs. Carter and Mrs. Hunt.

"Oh, nothing a-tall," Corinth answered airily. "I just shot a bear."

"Shot a bear!" exclaimed Mrs. Hunt. She looked in astonishment from the bear to her daughter and back to the bear.

"Your daughter saved Mr. Matheny from a horrible death," Mr. Carter explained. "Shot the critter while the rest of us stood around with our mouths open."

Mrs. Hunt hugged the girl and smiled at the others, as she said, "She's a wonderful shot, but I wish she'd learned to sew and cook as girls are supposed to do."

"Never again will I sew and cook," Corinth laughed. "I'm going to be a bear hunter from now on!"

When Mr. Matheny's wagon was fixed, the three vehicles rode on and caught up with the train before darkness. The following day they were out of the South Pass. Their trail led now to Fort Bridger, where supplies were bought and wagons once again checked. They pushed on as fast as possible northwestward toward Fort Hall. August was drawing to a close. They had to reach Oregon before the cold weather caught them.

At Soda Springs the emigrants stopped to rest and drink the carbonated waters. The Hunts ate their noonday meal away from the train at one of these springs. Jeff dipped up the cold, bubbling water and handed the tin cup to his mother, "Here, Ma, drink to wealth and prosperity in—"

He paused, gazing at his mother's face. Then he finished his sentence, "—in Oregon or California."

Mrs. Hunt said nothing. She took the cup and drank. "I can't stand much of that," she remarked, handing the cup back. "It bubbles up in my nose."

"Ma," Corinth asked in a subdued voice, "haven't you decided where we're going yet?"

Mrs. Hunt shook her head. She handed Corinth a plate of dried beef and apple butter and bread. "I don't have to decide finally until we reach Fort Hall," she told them. "Mr. Chiles and his California emigrants separate from the Oregon settlers there."

She passed a plate of food to Jeff, adding, "I don't want to talk about it now. I know you wish to go to Oregon and I know all too well your reasons. At Fort Hall I'll give you my decision."

Mrs. Hunt looked at their solemn faces and laughed. "Come, children, it's not all that bad," she joked. "Eat up and for dessert you can have soda water flavored with the juice from my preserved peaches."

They ate then. Jeff lay watching the leaves of the quaking aspen, turning and twisting in the breeze. It was fall already, for the aspen leaves were turning yellow. "Fall, and maybe headed for California," he thought sadly. "Oh, Pa, if we only knew whether you were alive."

"Listen," spoke Corinth. "There goes old Steamboat Springs."

Near by there was a deep, rumbling noise. "It sounds exactly like those steamboats we heard crossing the Mississippi River," Mrs. Hunt remarked.

That had been three years ago, Jeff remembered. Long ago and far away to the east. And Oregon far away to the west. Here he sat between, while his mother planned their future. He sighed. Waiting was the hardest work in the world. He wished they were at Fort Hall right now.

Five days later the Oregon Company reached Fort Hall. Coming out of the hot mountain valleys, the whitewashed walls of the fort looked cool and inviting across the desert. A red flag with white letters, H.B.C., flew from the two-story blockhouse. Here marked the end of the United States, for this was a British trading fort belonging to the Hudson Bay Company. From here to the Pacific coastline of Oregon, the United States and Great Britain occupied the country together.

Captain John Grant, the commander of the fort, welcomed the American citizens. He offered to trade good oxen for their sore-footed beasts and to

sell them food supplies. He also told them the discouraging news that wagons could not get past Fort Hall, for there was no road.

That night at supper Corinth asked her brother, "Doesn't our guide know the way into the Oregon country?"

"John Gantt has left us," Jeff told her. "He was hired to guide only to Fort Hall. I heard Mr. Applegate say today that no wagons have ever gone on from here to the Oregon coast."

"Doesn't Dr. Whitman know the way?" asked Corinth. "He's been a missionary to Oregon so long, surely he knows."

"He's not here and the men don't know where he has gone," answered Jeff.

Mrs. Hunt sighed. "It's very discouraging. Some are even turning back. Many of those who had planned to go to Oregon now are going to California."

She smiled a little sadly at Jeff. "I'm afraid we must give up hope of ever seeing your father again, children. That man who claimed to know him said he lived at the Devil's Gullet. I've asked and asked at every stop and no one's ever heard of the Devil's Gullet. I think the man lied because he knew you were anxious to hear good news. The pistol that hunter had only proves what I've been afraid of, that Indians killed Jim."

She paused and Jeff could see tears in her eyes. Then she went on. "Under the circumstances, I think we might as well go to California. We can get there in wagons and Mr. Chiles promised me he would give you work in his mill, Jeff. He's carrying all the mill machinery in his wagons."

Jeff stared at Corinth. She sighed and turned away from him. Jeff felt sick inside. His mother had decided to go to California and there was nothing he or Corinth could do or say to change her. Her reasons were good. But now he'd never know about his father.

CHAPTER THIRTEEN

Marcus Whitman Shows the Way

THE following day Jeff wandered gloomily among the wagons, listening to the talk.

"I aim to take my family and go back to Indiana," one man was saying. "I don't know why I ever left that good farm I had."

"I wouldn't go back over the way we've come for three farms in Indiana," remarked another. "I'll go on to Oregon if I have to foot it."

"Looks like you'll be footing it alone," the other man said. "Most of the folks are too discouraged to go on. They're turning back or going to California."

Jeff walked off to where several men sat around a fire, drinking coffee and talking.

"I tell you," one said, "that foreign red flag flying over Fort Hall is the reason we got to go on, wagon trail or no wagon trail."

A man got up and poured himself a cup of coffee from the pot hanging over the fire. "What do you mean?" he asked.

"I think all this country from the Atlantic straight across the continent to the Pacific ought to belong to the United States," the other explained. "Britain should give up her claim to all land below the 49th parallel."

"I agree with that," still another remarked. "And I'm willing to try to go on to Oregon. I hear the Willamette River Valley is the best farming land on this continent. And if we get more settlers in Oregon than the British, that good land will be ours, free for the taking and holding."

Jeff looked at the red flag flapping over the blockhouse roof and sighed. It wasn't his fight. He wasn't going to Oregon now. He'd never have a chance to settle on a fine big farm and claim it for his home country.

He walked away from the group of men. For a moment he paused at the outer edge of the camp, staring off at the winding Snake River. That river went to Oregon. It wound off through the mountains to the west.

He turned away sadly. He'd set his heart on finding his father, on living in Oregon. Now both these dreams were gone.

Making his way back to his own wagon, he heard a woman say, "California's got the best climate in the world."

"Who cares?" muttered Jeff and went on. He found Corinth sewing up a tear in her dress. He sat down beside her. "Do you think there is any possible way to change Ma's mind?" he asked.

Corinth bit off the thread before she answered, "There might be, but I don't know what it is."

But Corinth did have a plan. She didn't want to tell Jeff. It might not work. Or Jeff might ridicule it. She had heard that the missionary, Dr. Marcus Whitman, was returning the next day to Fort Hall. She was going to talk to him and beg him to see Mrs. Hunt to convince her that Oregon was the place for them to go.

Marcus Whitman did return the following afternoon. When he found out how discouraged the emigrants were, he called a meeting. He stood on a wagon tongue and spoke.

"Friends, I have heard that Captain Grant has told you that wagons have never made the journey into the Oregon country. It's true."

Several of the listeners groaned aloud.

The missionary held up his hand. "But wait! Captain Grant is British. He wants Oregon for Great Britain. And if you turn back, the British will have Oregon," he went on.

"Oregon for Americans!" shouted a man.

There were cries of, "On to Oregon!" and "Kick the British out!"

When the shouting had died down, Whitman continued, "I tell you that wagons *can* reach Oregon and I will guide you there. I know the way. It's not easy going, but the way will be no more difficult than what you have already been over."

Jeff hoped this speech would change his mother's attitude, but it didn't. "Mr. Chiles is leaving tomorrow, Jeff. Get the wagon in good shape," Mrs. Hunt commanded when they had returned to their wagon.

Jeff nodded. He wished a miracle would happen. He wished he'd never come west. He wished Jim Hunt would walk into camp.

"Oh, what's the use?" he asked himself and

began to unload the wagon so he could grease the wheels. He looked around for his sister. "She might at least help with the work," he grunted.

But Corinth was making her way to the missionary's tent. She paused a moment outside, biting her lip. Suppose he wouldn't listen to her? Suppose he—

She stopped, thinking, "There's no way of telling what he'll do till I ask him and find out."

She stepped into the opening and called in a low voice, "Dr. Whitman."

The missionary was seated at a table inside. He laid down his quill pen and glanced up. "Yes," he answered in a pleasant voice. "Come in."

Corinth stepped in and walked to the table. "I'm Corinth Hunt," she began uncertainly. Then before she knew it, she was telling this kindly looking man all about her father, all about how much she and Jeff wanted to go to Oregon, and about her mother's reluctance.

When she finished, the missionary smiled. "First," he said, "let me tell you that I have never heard of Jim Hunt in Oregon. But Oregon is being settled fast and I do not meet all of the people. But

I do know of the Devil's Gullet. It's the dangerous rapids in the Columbia River. Most people call it the Dalles."

Corinth clasped her hands. This was good news! "But will you come and talk to my mother?" she begged.

He stood up, his blue eyes twinkling. "There's no time like the present," he told her. "Let's go."

Corinth led the way to their wagon. Mrs. Hunt was repacking the few dishes she had brought with them. She looked at the two in surprise.

"Mrs. Hunt, your daughter has told me your troubles," Dr. Whitman began. "I do not mean to pry into your affairs. But may I urge you to come on to Oregon with us?"

Mrs. Hunt glanced at her daughter coldly. "Corinth knows I have already decided not to go to Oregon." She emphasized the *not*.

Dr. Whitman nodded. "She told me. But let me hasten to tell you that the Devil's Gullet is in Oregon and that your husband might well be there," he said.

Mrs. Hunt listened while the missionary went on to tell her of Oregon and its advantages as a place to live. He assured her that if the Indians had killed her husband, he would have heard about it at his mission. He offered to help her search for Jim Hunt, to let her live at the mission while they looked for him.

Then he turned toward Jeff and added, "Oregon offers limitless opportunities for a hard-working boy like yours, Mrs. Hunt. I remember how he handled his team of mules across the Platte River. He'll have no trouble taking care of you in Oregon."

Mrs. Hunt looked off into the distance. What should she do? Dr. Whitman had given her the first real hope she'd had that her husband might be alive. He would be a good friend to have and would be a great help in the search for Jim.

She turned back and said, "All right, Dr. Whitman, I will change my mind, which is the full right of every woman." She smiled at her children as she added, "We will go on to Oregon."

"Yippeee! On to Oregon!" yelled Jeff. Corinth jumped up and down in excitement.

When the missionary had left, Jeff said, "Corinth, you're the best sister in the world. You're a bear-killer. You're an Oregon ring-tailed roarer, a rip-snorting yellow flower of the frontier!" He grabbed Corinth and danced around the wagon with her.

Mrs. Hunt said soberly, "Jeff, I guess I really had no idea it meant so much to you to go to Oregon."

Jeff dropped Corinth's hands. "It does, Ma. 'Cause I know Pa's alive. I know he is!" he said emphatically. "And Ma, even if we don't find him there, I promise you, you won't suffer. I'll work hard on our farm."

"Yippee! On to Oregon!" yelled Jeff

"Me too!" cried Corinth. "And don't you remember what Dr. Whitman told us? Whatever we
do for ourselves in Oregon, we're doing for our
country too, because we're helping Oregon become
part of America."

"I know you'll work hard," Mrs. Hunt answered
with a smile. "I'm proud of both of you. Now let's
hurry and get the wagon ready for the rest of the
journey. We must get to Oregon before the British
take it."

The following morning the Mathenys told the
Hunts good-by. The old farmer and his wife were
heading southward toward California with the
Chiles' wagon train. Soon after that group had
gone, the Oregon emigrants left too. Marcus
Whitman led the way in a two-wheeled oxcart,
making a trail for the others to follow.

They followed the Snake River along the south
bank day after day through the same bleakness of
earth and sky and sun. On they went through an
arid land of sagebrush and bunch grass and lizards,
where the coyotes howled the livelong night.

"Corinth," Jeff said one day. "Don't tell Ma, but
the mules are giving out. This desert country is
hard on 'em."

"Maybe you'd better buy some corn from that man who offered it," Corinth suggested.

Jeff nodded. "I will," he agreed. "There's no forage along here for 'em. I'll just have to give them more corn."

The train crossed the Snake River and pushed on through more bleak landscape to Fort Boisé. Here they crossed the Snake again, heading for the Blue Mountains. They went slowly through the Burnt River Canyon, a narrow valley filled with huge trees.

Still they struggled on and by the beginning of October were among the pines and firs and hemlocks of the Grande Ronde River. Dr. Whitman left the group here to hurry ahead to his mission. He chose a trusted Indian to guide the emigrants.

When they reached the Whitman mission on the Walla Walla River, ten days later, Mrs. Hunt told the children, "We'll stay here till we find your father."

But Dr. Whitman urged her to go on. "Mrs. Hunt," he said, "you'd better go with the other settlers to the Devil's Gullet. If you don't find your husband there, you can return here to the mission with my Indian guide."

Downstream from the mission was Fort Walla Walla, belonging to the Hudson Bay Company. Here the emigrants split up. A part went on in wagons along the Columbia River with the cattle. The rest built boats to complete the journey by water.

"I don't believe I can ride another minute in this swaying, bumping wagon," Mrs. Hunt told Jeff. "See if we can go downstream with the Carter family."

"I'm not sad to leave the wagon either, Ma," Corinth said.

It was agreed that Val and Jeff and Mr. Carter would build a raft. They paid one of the other families to drive their mules and oxen to the Dalles. When all the boats were completed, the fleet floated off down the Columbia.

Jeff and Val and Corinth sat on the bundles in the middle of the boat, watching the shoreline. "Hooray for Oregon," Jeff declared happily. "This is the kind of river I like. A wide, clear stream with trees along the banks."

Val nodded and added, "This is certainly the most beautiful river we've seen on our journey."

It was wonderful not to have to ride in the jolting wagons. The cool fresh air smelled clean and delicious to Corinth. "This is one trail that won't ever get dusty!" she cried.

At nights they tied up on shore, camping among huge pine trees. Once they traded with Indians who had shells and bones stuck through holes pierced in their noses. Then one day Corinth pointed ahead of them. "Oh, look!" she exclaimed.

"That snow-capped mountain. See it, Jeff?"

It was Mount Hood, its white cap floating mysteriously above the green woods before them.

"Mountains and rivers and woods," Val remarked. "This Oregon is my country."

One morning their guide told them that they would reach the rapids of the Columbia in a few hours. "Is that the Devil's Gullet?" Mrs. Hunt asked.

The guide nodded. Jeff was excited. Soon, perhaps, they would see his father! "Let me steer the boat this morning," he begged.

Mr. Carter laughed. "It won't go any faster for

you than it will for me," he said. "But I know you are anxious to reach the Devil's Gullet."

The river flowed wide and smooth here. Jeff had no trouble steering the raft. But about mid-morning the voyagers heard a great roaring from ahead.

Jeff was caught off balance

"It's the rapids of the Columbia," shouted Val.

Jeff stared curiously ahead. What would the Devil's Gullet look like? Would there be houses? And what if Jim Hunt was not here?

And suddenly there it was before them. Great cliffs of black rock on each side of the river, so close together that it seemed impossible for a boat to get between them.

Jeff could see the water froth and whirl dangerously through the narrow channel. "It's well named," he thought.

The guide in the wooden dugout at the front motioned the fleet toward the south bank. Jeff stood at the rear and turned the steering paddle, swinging the raft in that direction. Suddenly the raft hit an unseen rock. There was a grinding crash and one side of the boat tilted sharply.

Jeff was caught off balance. He threw out his arms, trying to catch himself. But he was falling—falling into the worst rapids in the Columbia River!

CHAPTER FOURTEEN

From Sea to Shining Sea

THE icy water was a sudden paralyzing shock to Jeff's body. It numbed his arms and legs. Down he went, unable to move. A great pain burned in his chest. He had to have air!

He kicked weakly. His heavy shoes dragged his feet down. His shirt bound his arms. He felt himself sink slowly. His ears roared. His lungs were bursting. He was drowning!

Then he lashed the water with his arms and legs, fighting his way to the surface with great effort. He sucked in great chestfuls of air. But the river was choppy and it was all he could do to keep his head above the water. The current tugged strongly at him. His shoes weighed a ton. His head slipped beneath the surface again.

"Help me, God!" he cried to himself. "Don't let me drown now we're finally in Oregon."

Once again he struggled to the surface. He kicked his feet and worked his arms. A wave lapped over him. He was whirling around in the swift water, headed into the Devil's Gullet. "I'm a goner," he thought wildly.

At that moment a rope fell across the water beside him. He reached out his hand but couldn't find it. Something washed against his shoulder and he grabbed at it. It was the rope.

As he gripped it with both hands, he found himself being pulled slowly through the water. The current tore at him. One hand slipped. He strained to hold on, but his fingers were stiff and cold. He couldn't hold another minute. The rope was easing out of his grasp.

Then strong hands grabbed him and pulled him into a dugout. Jeff lay in the bottom of the boat, gasping and spluttering. He was weak and tired and half-drowned. The boat reached the bank and he was lifted out to the ground. He lay there with his eyes closed. He heard the Carters and his mother and sister come up.

"Is he dead?" asked Corinth.

At that moment Jeff opened his eyes and tried to grin. Corinth helped him to sit up. He looked around at the white faces and said, "Oregon water tastes a heap better than other water, but there wasn't any need of me making a hog of myself and drinking so much."

Mr. Carter laughed. Mrs. Hunt began to thank the Indian guide who had saved her son's life. Corinth told him that no one else had been thrown off the raft and that all the boats were lined up safely along the shore.

Jeff looked around him. There were a few cabins back among the pines. And higher up the hillside was a mission. He wondered if his father lived in one of the cabins. He changed into dry clothes behind a rock.

A lean, tanned man in buckskins emerged from the woods and limped down the hillside toward the group. He was a tall man. Jeff stared at him curiously. There was something familiar about him.

Suddenly he screamed, "Pa! It's Pa!"

He ran up the slope toward the man. But Cor-

There was something familiar about the man

inth shot past him and threw herself into her father's arms.

"Pa, we thought you were dead! And the Indian had your pistol! And I killed a grizzly! And a mountain man said . . ."

Mr. Hunt grinned delightedly as he clapped his hand over her mouth. "I'd plumb forgot Corinth could talk such a blue streak," he laughed, hugging the little girl.

Jeff had run back to help his mother. Mrs. Hunt had turned very pale and looked as though she might faint.

Mr. Hunt hurried toward her. "Kate!" he cried happily as he took her in his arms.

Mrs. Hunt burst into tears. But in a minute she was smiling as all four of them tried to hug each other at the same time. "Oh, Jim, we thought you were dead!" she cried.

The Carters came up to be introduced. Mr. Hunt shook hands with them.

"You come on up to my cabin," he invited. "We have lots to tell each other. And I know Corinth is dying to begin where she left off a moment ago." He winked at his daughter and led the way up the hillside.

They reached a log cabin. Over the porch was a sign with letters burned into the wood. It said:

HUNT'S STORE.

"Pa! You got a store!" Corinth exclaimed in amazement.

"I had to do something while I was crippled," he replied. He went on to explain, "I broke my leg and couldn't travel back east for you. So I decided while I waited for you to come here, I could do a little trading. This has always been a place where the Indians came to trade, at the head of these rapids, the Dalles, or Devil's Gullet, as we call it. I have heard that Lewis and Clark stopped here to trade with the redskins in 1805."

"But have you given up farming?" asked Jeff.

"I have," his father answered. "But you haven't. I have a farm staked out for you in the Willamette River Valley. The Willamette flows into the Columbia River some distance downstream from here."

"That's where most of the emigrants are going," Mr. Carter remarked.

"It's the richest soil in Oregon," Mr. Hunt said. "But I mustn't keep you here admiring my store. Come around to the back where I live."

Mr. Hunt led the way to a cabin behind the store. He threw open the door. "Welcome!" he cried.

A fire burned in the big stone fireplace. The

emigrants seated themselves, and **Mr.** Hunt took a
pot of coffee from over the wood embers.

"You'll need something to warm you up. Oregon winters are mild, but sometimes damp."

"Jeff found that out," Val laughed. "The Columbia River is very damp, isn't it, Jeff?"

Jeff grinned, but turned to his father. "Why didn't you send us a letter, Pa?" he asked.

Mr. Hunt looked at his son in amazement. "But I did, Jeff," he replied. "Didn't you get it?"

"No, we didn't, Jim," Mrs. Hunt said. "As I told you, I thought you were dead. And if it hadn't been for the children, we'd be in California right now with the Mathenys."

"Why, I sent a letter east by a trader," Mr. Hunt explained. "It was right after I broke my leg. I had very little money and the man admired my pistol. So I gave him the weapon, and he agreed to take the letter."

"The trader must have been killed by the Indians then," Jeff interrupted. "For your pistol was taken from a dead Sioux by a mountain man. I saw it and was afraid you'd been killed and the gun taken from you."

Then Mr. Hunt sliced some cold venison, and with coffee and bread they ate dinner. When the meal was over, Corinth told her father about shooting the grizzly. Later, each told of the hardships of the Oregon Trail.

Mr. Hunt nodded. "Hard on you, I know it must have been," he agreed. "But let me tell you something you don't know yet, but will shortly find out. This Oregon land is well worth any hardships you've gone through."

He looked around the room at each of the faces and added, "And I'm glad to see more American settlers in Oregon. The British want to take this country from us."

"I've heard that we have as much right to Oregon as the British," Mr. Carter spoke.

"It's true," Mr. Hunt told him. "Captain Robert Gray, an American trader from Boston, discovered and named the Columbia River in 1792. This was before Lieutenant Broughton of the British Navy explored it."

"That seems decisive enough for us to claim the land," Mr. Carter said.

"It does seem that way to me," Mr. Hunt replied. "Though the British say their traders and trappers settled here in Oregon long before John Jacob Astor established his trading post at Astoria in 1811. But Astoria was the first permanent settlement made here. Americans made it, so that's another point in our favor."

"Looks like we'll have to flip a coin for the country," Corinth remarked.

"Not if Americans continue to come to Oregon to live," Mr. Hunt went on. "Possession is nine-tenths of the law, I've always heard, and I believe it'll be that way here. If folks'll just keep coming over the Oregon Trail, we'll get this land. Not many Britishers are willing to leave their homes and settle here."

"Well, everyone is talking about Oregon in the States," Jeff told his father. "Marcus Whitman made a trip to Washington, and even as far away as Boston, to tell everybody about this country."

"That's right, Mr. Hunt, everybody is interested," Mr. Carter agreed. "President John Tyler doesn't seem to care about the Oregon country. But I heard before I left Missouri last spring that James K. Polk is very much interested in this country and is going to run for President in 1844. They say Polk wants all of Oregon or none."

"I agree with him entirely," Mr. Hunt remarked vigorously. "Russia has renounced all claims to land south of the parallel of 54 degrees and 40 minutes. And by the Florida Treaty of 1819, Spain gave up any claim to this country."

"So that only leaves the British?" Jeff asked.

"Yes," Mr. Hunt answered. "But the British are determined to have this fine country. And they are a powerful nation."

"You mean they might fight for Oregon?" asked Corinth.

"They might," Mr. Hunt answered. "But I believe if we get lots of American citizens here in Oregon, they'll let us have the country peacefully."

"That's what Dr. Whitman believes," Mrs. Hunt added.

"Dr. Whitman believes like the rest of us who are living here," Mr. Hunt told them. "We all believe that the American title to Oregon is clear and unquestionable. Not just a portion of this country but a clear and unquestionable title to *all* of Oregon."

"Hooray for Oregon!" Val yelled. He turned to his friend. "Jeff, we may have to fight for our rights. And we'll whip those British for the third time."

"Let's hope we don't have to fight," Mrs. Carter remarked fervently. "War is terrible."

"It is," agreed her husband. "But this land from the Atlantic to the Pacific ought to be ours. And if we have to fight for it, we will. Oregon for Americans, I say!"

"I feel as if it's ours," Mrs. Hunt put in. "We went through dust and heat and many hard times to get here. And from what I heard in Independence, I don't think our great emigration of 1843 will be the last. I expect more and more Americans will come out here every year, in spite of all the hardships and dangers."

"Push on west and see the sights, my father always said," Mr. Hunt laughed. "He did just that by going to Kentucky. Now I've done the same by coming to Oregon."

"But that leaves no place west of here for Jeff and me to go," Corinth wailed. "What can we do?"

"We can swim in the Pacific Ocean," Jeff grinned. "It's ours now. Hooray for Oregon!"

Jeff and Val separated, promising to visit each other every year if they didn't have to fight. And they didn't. After these first brave pioneers who followed the Oregon Trail, more and more settlers came to Oregon. And in 1846 a treaty was signed by Great Britain, giving up most of the land south of the 49th degree parallel. Jeff and Corinth and

Val and all the others who traveled the Oregon Trail had helped to make the United States a continental nation—a land of democracy from coast to coast, from sea to shining sea.

About the Author

WILLIAM O. STEELE lives in Tennessee, on Lookout Mountain, from which, usually, seven states can be seen. Mr. Steele says that on a clear day the Oregon Trail can also be seen. His three children deny this, but they agree that their father has shown a clear picture of the exciting life on the Trail in WE WERE THERE ON THE OREGON TRAIL. He has written many other books about America's historical past, among them, THE STORY OF DANIEL BOONE; FRANCIS MARION, YOUNG SWAMP FOX; and WINTER DANGER.

About the Illustrator

JO POLSENO lives in Westport, Connecticut, with his wife and three children. He put in three years of combat in Europe, four years studying fine arts, and has had numerous jobs that have given him valuable experience in his career as an artist. He has done advertising art work, designed book jackets, and illustrated books for several publishers. He is now an instructor at the Famous Artist Course in Westport.

About the Historical Consultant

RAY IRWIN was born in Missouri, where his family has lived for generations not far from Independence, jumping-off place for pioneers making the journey along the Oregon Trail. After finishing college there, he went on to graduate work at the University of California and the University of Chicago. He received his doctorate from New York University where he is now Associate Professor of History. He is now at work on a book about the westward movement in America. He and his wife spend their summers working on their farm in southwest Missouri.